Scrutineer Publishing

By the same author

The Book of Dirt

The Carving Circle

Gretchen Heffernan

First published 2017
Scrutineer Publishing
www.scrutineer.org
info@scrutineer.org

Book and Cover Design:
The Scrutineer, Rachael Adams.
Fonts: Adobe Garamond, Bree serif.
Printed and bound by IngramSpark, on 50lb
uncoated paper.

SCB Distributors
15608 South New Century Drive,
Gardena, CA 90248
United States of America

ISBN: 978-0-9956843-7-9

Acknowledgements

A heartfelt thank you to Arcadians everywhere, in particular, Rachael Adams for her support and shimmering brilliance.

Dedication

All the words are for Mike.

The Humours Quartet
Book One: Black Bile, The Carving Circle

Prologue

The first thing Jacques Beaumont brought back to life was a field mouse. He was just a boy and had found the mouse dead near the woodshed. It was in perfect condition, as though it had simply keeled over and stopped breathing. The creature seemed unconscious and when he picked it up, he half expected it to wake and bite him, but it just lay in his palm like a bit of stiff pelt. He couldn't believe his luck. It was perfect for carving. He had a block of pine in his bedroom, already smooth and soft as toffee, just waiting for this mouse and his chisel, as if the two were fated, which, he'd eventually come to understand, they were.

He ran up the stairs to his bedroom. The room was hot and breezeless, even with the window open, and he began to sweat as he laid the mouse carefully inside a towel-lined box. Every corner of the room was cluttered with animal bones, rocks, snakeskins, beetle casings, feathers, eye knots of wood and sketchbooks like a dragon's hoard of found things he loved to carve.

He studied the mouse's body before he placed the box on his desk and took up his chisel. The mouse was the first mammal he had ever carved and he wanted it to be faultless. It took him hours to replicate the mouse's delicate features accurately, and he lost all sense of time in the process, yet when he'd finished, the mouse and the figurine were, in essence, identical. He looked at his work in admiration. Focus had seemed to melt into his hands, as though his hands were acting extraneously from his body, yet somewhere close, though distant in feeling, like the future. He held the figurine lovingly to his chest and the mouse's legs began to scratch against the cardboard. He peered hesitantly into the box, where he watched, with incredulousness, as the rest of the mouse's body softened and twitched to life.

Quickly, he tipped the box on its side and the mouse hurried out. The carving seemed to seethe to a fizz in his hand and he looked at it in wonder. Could it have had something to do with the mouse's revival? Resurrection was not a term he understood then, and everything he felt was based on a bewildered sort of reflex. The roar of a coming wave flooded his ears, his mind and vision.

Before he could think another thought, the mouse ran across his desk and quickly leapt out of the window, plummeting to a second death. He could see the dark splat of its small body like a squashed grape against the ground below, and as he gripped the carving in his hand, he found that he knew, instinctively, how to will the mouse alive. He squeezed and prayed and slowly, as though blowing up a tiny balloon, the mouse's body began to take form. It stood, dazed and bloodied, but very much alive, and ran away.

In that moment, time revealed its fluctuating existence to Jacques. How the power of the mind, when released from the body, from the myth of identity, can overlap time and that no thing, shape, or idea is ever truly static or linear. In fact, fervent living takes place where time overlaps and it was inside such a space that he met Elora.

There are people in the world that direct this alteration and there are people in the world that simply adjust. Jacques was one of the directors, as was Elora, and when he resurrects her into her full reawakening, she will realize how much he loved her and loves her still.

*

Jacques walks into his garage and flicks on the light. The slender trunk of pine is resting like a patient on his workbench. He removes the sheet with the flair of a magician. I'll begin with the head, he thinks. Its shape and hair; I'll save her face for last. Elora's features had always been exquisite. He would have to choose her expression carefully and he hoped that by carving her body first, her form might explain her desired countenance. It's important that she has a choice, he doesn't want her to feel forced or manipulated, so he listens to the wood and the life still inside it akin to a faint heartbeat.

He begins to tear away each piece of her bark as though it were a fresh scab. He uses his hands and a small chisel. Anything electric, he fears, might jolt her and that is not what the wood wants. She's alive, but he needs to build her emotions and for creating her persona he relies on listening to the wood.

He delicately turns her over and peels the bark from her other side. She is the length of a head and torso. He runs his hands down the cylinder of her figure, a gesture so intimate that if she were awake, she'd shiver. The wood splinters where it's knotted, like a folded knuckle, and he begins sanding her back to a smooth, honeyed bone.

There is an initial sense of mutilation that remains until the sculpture has come to life, not alive in the way that blood knows it, but life as resurrection through smell, through touch, and that captured narrative we screw into ourselves to hold our memories together. Once they grasp that his purpose is to remake them as solid and strong, his marks move from scars to inscriptions and the relationship begins.

He has loved them all. Truly. He looks across the valley dotted with his sculptures and watches the sun lower below the mountaintop like the yellow arc of a reptilian eye closing the mountain gray. Each one of them a different character of Elora, each one, designing her memory. More than love. Love when it's explosive.

He sands her down with long raspy sighs. The wood underneath is fresh and perfect and untouched. I'll keep the first piece I chisel out of her, he thinks, curled as a child's tendril, I'll keep it close to me.

He's been saving this piece of wood for Elora for nearly a year. He's felt her waiting, tiptoeing like a cat, along the periphery of his creative view. He labels each log with a date and place of discovery and files them in his woodshed. He has it all planned. This sculpture will focus on carving her head, chest and waist. She will have two metal posts for legs, as he perfected her legs on another sculpture months ago, and a floor-length nightdress composed of wooden medallions, each engraved with a symbol.

He'll drill a hole in the top and bottom of each medallion and fasten them together with wire, like chainmail. She'll stand in the garden with her emblem nightdress circling around her. She'll have a view of the mountains and the others to keep her company, until she completely turns.

Until she comes back to him.

In the beginning, during his activation, the time that he now thinks of as the period when he was learning how to resurrect, his sculpting was frenzied and raw. He'd race through forms that were often muddled with misshapen animals, digging, cutting through layers to get to the bottom of himself. Now, each new sculpture arrives as an instruction of crystalline precision that he can feel expanding beneath his eyelids like frost.

He understands how wood is perfect for re-embodiment and invites touch because it, too, is cellular and composed of tissues, so cell attracts cell and regrows cell. It burns, its wounds leak, and it has a memory and turns to stone, like our bones, when they're petrified, yet retains a warmth that is unduplicated. He understands this warmth, like the warmth of a human, comes from the sharpening or growing of a core, and must first endure tools, both brutal and smoothing, such as life. Such as age, how time quickly possesses cellular entities, so the perfect sculpture, like a human, begins to erode as soon as it's created, for the earth lays claims to the reusing of molecules from the beginning. He understands how all molecules are intelligent, yet fluctuating, and therein lies their precious ability to mutate. His sculptures merely restructure this mutation.

Jacques's maman, his father and now Jacques himself were all born with the ability to harness life's forces. We are taught the laws of physics and, without question, these influence our universe, but the forces that dominate our species are the laws of emotional acumen. Jacques's lineage understood that physics and intelligence could be interchangeably influenced through ritualistic prayer. Sculpture is his form of prayer; his father's was photography; his maman's was Voodoo.

It is an old wisdom and Jacques was born into it.

*

He picks up a wooden medallion from the kitchen table, places it inside of his palm and opens and closes his hand like a blinking eye. He used to dream that he had eyes in his hands. What would she say? What would she want said? He feels that what she wants, what is missing, is a story. I'll give you my own, he thought, and unite it with yours.

Some nights the frost behind his eyes suffocates him. It weaves one pattern furiously over the other, until it grows into a single block of ice that he has to crack himself out of. He walks through his mind then, breaking open his sculptures with a hammer and chisel. His past bursts from their wooden skulls like trapped black flies.

He remembers now.

That summer there had been a plague of bluebottles. He remembers everything. He sits down at the table and begins sketching a fly, a bear, an onion, a pint of jam, mountains. A young woman who loved to sing. Elora. A river. A bird. A murder. A story.

1.

Pine Creek, Ontario 1933 - 1953

Mathis Beaumont was a photographer because he needed a layer between himself and his obsession with grizzly bears. It worked like glue inside a crack. It united and divided the fact that he was both man and bear. The lens allowed him to filter. It wasn't until after Mathis had disappeared, that Jacques began to fully comprehend the use of his father's filter and how you can grow one, like an invisible fingernail, in order to tolerate yourself.

Their house had stood in a valley of mountains like a block of soap inside a green dish. It was a two-story rectangle of worn clapboard. The lake beside it was completely still and reflected another house, watery and surreal, like a parallel world that he could jump into. This was the view, the dimension, his mother preferred, and in the spring, when it was clear that she was ill and wasn't recovering, she moved her chair to the window and watched the mountains tremor in the water, as though working up the courage to stare at the real thing. Hibernating season was over and his father was away.

"You've got to chew the fruit to see the pit," she told Jacques, speaking of his father's absence. "His expeditions are the closest he gets to chewing himself. Passion is like that. Like chewing yourself. That's the way it is with people. I didn't choose him. You think I'd *choose* a lunatic? Lord, no, he just happened upon me. And he didn't choose that blasted bear. She was just always his. And it's true your father's half mad, but let me tell you something, he feels fear and he loves anyway, and that's a darn sight better then fearing nothing and loving nothing and living half dead. You got that? Half mad is better living than half dead."

She looked out the window towards the row of pines that wrapped around the base of the mountain and protected their valley from the cold rock. She picked a piece of loose thread from her cardigan and rolled it between her thumb and forefinger. It was one of her lucid moments and he sat beside her on the sofa. She reached over and put her hand on his knee.

"But not you, no. You've got the look of the hell bent."

She looked out the window again. The pines were dark frayed knees against a denim horizon. The sun was low and golden in the sky.

"It'll snow," she said. "It'll snow before the week's out. It may be April, but I know the goddamn weather."

She took his hand and stroked it as though he were a small child.

"Someday," she said and he sat waiting for her to continue.

Geese were calling fourth the spring and his heart sank at their freedom.

"Someday you'll have a bear and it will eat you," she sighed. "Or you'll chase it," she sighed, "but probably both."

And so.

The thought that he might be full of real and imaginary bears was an idea that Jacques carefully folded up and placed inside his heart like a note inside an envelope.

*

Mathis Beaumont's unusual affection for bears could be traced back to his devotion to a particular *ushanka*, also known as a Russian trapper's hat. It was a wild and magnificent possession for a child living in the south of France. One could argue that the hat saved the emotional life of young Mathis Beaumont, for even as a grown man, he could close his eyes and glaze the boy he once was until that child shined bright enough for Mathis to feel a soft fur against his eyelids. Indeed it was the fur that made the hat truly wonderful. It was stitched from the hide of a Russian *Urrissi* bear, a distant relative of the North American grizzly, and gave Mathis the warmth he would eventually use to draw the line his life would follow.

But before that, others drew it for him.

Mathis was the illegitimate child of General Jean Philippe Beaumont, a French nobleman with a preference for Haitian women. The year was 1905 and two things happened that irrevocably transformed Mathis's future: his mother, a beautiful Creole housekeeper, died and Jean Philippe Beaumont was diagnosed with syphilis.

In a desperate act to save his soul, as well as rejuvenate his marred member, Jean Phillippe moved his illegitimate son to his least favorite countryside residence, Château de la Colline Pourpre, an hour east of Aix-en-Provence and a million miles away from the streets of Paris. Mathis was given a hot bath, a hot meal and a cold English governess.

However, despite his one act of kindness, Jean Philippe perished and Mathis, in accordance with French law, inherited his financial birthright. His stepmother was furious and immediately shipped him to a boarding school in Montreal, Canada, as far away from Parisian society as his passport allowed.

It was a dream come true for Mathis. He placed the *ushanka* on his head, boarded the ship, stood at the prow and watched the Atlantic shove them to Canada. Land of the Grizzlies. Two years later the world went to war, and Mathis, for the second time in his life, had been saved by another's vanity.

*

An particular fascination seldom exists without a sensible origin. General Jean Philippe had always refused Mathis cuddly toys because he claimed they were emasculating. His playthings were restricted to weapons, and while the governess wouldn't be so bold as to give Mathis a secret teddy, she did offer him the *ushanka* his father was given during a Russian post.

After dinner his governess would read from one of Jean Philippe's prescribed war novels and Mathis would snuggle up to his hat. They sat by the fire in the winter and on the terrace during the summer. Mathis listened and rubbed the hat across his cheeks. The fur dampened with his breath and soon grew matted inside his small, tight grip, and it was through this affection that his uncanny interest in grizzly bears grew.

This was an interest his father was happy to endorse, so that by the time Mathis left for Montreal, he was practically an expert on the subject. He saw his life as running parallel to the solitary and nomadic existence of the grizzly bear. After boarding school, he packed his camera equipment and made the long journey towards Ontario, where he bought a modest house in the middle of nowhere and began to pursue his passions in peace.

His love of photography did not have such obvious origins. It couldn't be pinpointed, but almost certainly dovetailed with his relationship to light. Light and its ability to replace words. Unspeakable, unfathomable words that stitched his memory with radiance. Indeed, his memory was held together with light. Candles in a room and his mother singing, dancing, praying. Men with lanterns in dark streets. A fire in a barrel. The cold moon through a crack in his bedroom ceiling and the glare of wet rocks against a cloudless sky. His mother lighting the desk lamp and the mountains moving from pink to purple like heavenly ships. He was a prism of his memory and in every direction he turned, light catalogued and defined him, so when his father gave him a Brownie camera for his birthday, it felt like the final benediction of an internal instrument that had long since been playing.

2

During his first few years in Pine Creek Mathis watched the light religiously and hardly spoke a word. He planted a garden. He read, and reread, the books he'd brought with him. He spent months away tracking, mapping and photographing the grizzlies in his area. He had pictures of them fishing, mating, clawing the earth and sleeping in large, soft piles. He grew accustomed to the smell of his body and the voice of his mind. It was like meeting an entirely new person. He knew hunger, danger and thirst. He watched the bear and learnt the mimicry of survival. He tended his garden and thought of himself as supremely happy.

But restlessness is the thorn of happiness, and one evening he found himself standing on the Nose, a boulder that jutted out from the rock face, and staring at the lit windows of a distant town.

The next morning he came down from the mountain and enquired about a room for the night. It was 1930 and the wheat prices had fallen so drastically that tens of thousands of farmers had been forced to leave their land. The country had gone into economic ruin and the innkeeper turned him away as though he were another vagrant until he produced cash from his wallet. The money was too much for the innkeeper to resist and he gave Mathis a room. From the window Mathis watched horses pull cars their owners could no longer afford to fuel. He saw entire families that were shoeless and begging. The sound of his voice had shocked him, but not so much as the desperation of humanity.

An hour and a clean face later, he trudged camera and tripod through the town, offering bread to those that would pose for him. He was told that the horse drawn cars were called Bennett Buggy's. Many of them had been turned into homes with blankets and the few household items the travellers could carry stashed away under ripped seats and inside glove boxes. He peered inside a car window and took a photo of a soiled child nursing from a breast like a small pillow of air pushing from a ribcage.

No one had the energy to complain. Their eyes reminded him of animals in the dead of winter. Many traded half the bread for drink, which was another form of hibernation and he learned to feed the children first.

When he could no longer endure what he was seeing, he walked to the edge of town and into the woods. He set up his tripod and camera forty feet away from an old Ponderosa with the intent of capturing something more alive than the life he'd just witnessed. Which is exactly what happened, because when he looked through the lens, he saw Nora, sitting at the base of the tree and staring straight at him. The lens had turned her upside down. He could see that she was brown and beautiful even on her head.

She walked towards him and pointed to the camera.

"I've heard of those. They say one can steal your soul," she said and stuck out her hand. "I'm Nora."

"Mathis," he shook her hand, "nice to meet you. Would you like to try it? It is not true about the soul stealing. I promise."

"I have a good grip anyway," she said and moved in front of the lens, looked through it and immediately lurched back. He caught her; it was like holding a deer in his arms. She pushed away from him and brushed herself off.

"Sorry," he laughed until he saw that she was not amused. "I should have told you the lens turns everything upside down," he said. "Try it again."

He felt her go quiet, so quiet that the silence between them became an understanding. She was chewing her tongue. He watched her and although she didn't move, she reflected a feeling of intrinsic life, like a tree trunk. She was small and steady. Industrious, he thought, a wren. Her whole body jolted and he heard the shutter snap. He looked in the direction of the photograph and saw nothing. She emerged from the focusing cloth with a smile.

"Perfect," she said and walked off into the trees. She lifted her muddy skirt and petticoat like a princess. He stared after her until she disappeared and then wondered if she'd been real. Strange things can happen to a lonely man, he thought, and then: Wait. Am I lonely?

Back in his dark room, weeks later, he watched the image of a small cardinal emerge from a dish of chemicals. It was sitting on a branch. Its chest was all puffed out as though it were just about to sing. So, he thought, not a wren after all. A cardinal. He spent the rest of the afternoon coloring its feathers red. The next day he framed and hung the photograph on the wall. It reminded him of snow before it's been stepped in.

Day after day the cardinal sang to him. He couldn't stop hearing it, so busied himself and made a stew. Venison, juniper berry, tarragon. He stirred the pot and noticed the hand that held the spoon did not resemble his own. It was as hard as dark grit stone. He stopped and took inventory of himself. His body was calloused and scarred, ugly even, but his mind, his inside felt remarkably supple, as though he'd become the perfect design of a clam.

Perhaps, he thought.

Perhaps that's the way it is with work that you love?

Perhaps a strong body, makes a strong mind that unfastens inside?

It begins with something small. An idea. A hat. Two cells. A cardinal in a tree. Yes, he thought, yes. He wanted to share this revelation with someone; he looked at the photograph hanging on the wall, and then at the mountain beyond. He tasted the stew, it wasn't ready yet, and there was time to weed and water his garden before dinner. He'd need a hot meal inside him for the two-day hike it'd take him to reach his bride. He never gave it a second thought.

He arrived in town on a Sunday. There was a market and the street was bustling with beggars, whores, greengrocers, businessmen and ladies. He found her right away. She was wearing a hat that shadowed half her face. Her clothes were not new, but they were clean. She stood next to a stall knocking on a watermelon to test its ripeness. When he asked her to live with him, she thought about how only his eyes and his mouth would be visible in the night. The fever had taken her entire family. She had just enough money to survive the year, and all thoughts beyond that accompanied a panic so great that she often wished for death. She said yes.

Their life was peaceful, until Mathis met Callisto and something inside him stepped from one room into another, entirely. He hadn't realized he'd been made of rooms. He'd spent all autumn and winter inside Nora and the house they inhabited. He whittled her two cats for the mantelpiece and made a wardrobe for her dresses. He carved swirls of wind on the banister and leaves on the woodwork. He hung up his photos of birds, at her eyelevel, not his, because he knew she liked them, yet, all the same, when spring arrived, the walls seemed to tighten.

There is no other way to keep me, he told her and left.

He tracked the female bear for days through trees heavy with vine. The ferns were waist high and the ground was wet and buggy. Her urine smelled like a woman's heat and he felt her around every corner, so strong was her presence, that birds startled him, so did the rain.

How could he have been so careless? His equipment was getting soaked. He walked back to his campsite, crawled inside and laid his camera out to dry. Rain fell and slid down the tarpaulin, while he sat grumbling and picking at things, a hair from his hat, dirt from his fingernail, fluff, finally, he got up and walked outside.

There she was.

A silver freight train of steam. Callisto reared up and he tasted the hot spray of her breath, saw her yellow teeth, her nostrils spat. What could he do?

He had a wild heart.

He felt a part of himself incinerate, every bit of him burned with sweat, the rattle of her spit sawed the air, and a crack between them, like wood catching fire, catching instinct, struck. The animal in him rose up to greet her; she lowered, grunted and walked away. It was terrifyingly simple. He named her Callisto, and when he returned in the autumn, Nora noticed that a part of his soul was, indeed, missing. It was the part that looked at her, only. He told her he'd been struck by lightning, but she knew photography had stolen him.

Over the years Mathis and Callisto came to resemble one another, as though his photographs were captured mirrors, so that by the time Jacques was a young boy, he couldn't think of his father without thinking of Callisto. The two seemed fixed together like a handshake, like an ancient pact.

*

In the mountains and at home in his darkroom, Mathis hunted. He was a hunter of light. A hunter of illumination, where nothing remained untouched.

When Nora told him that she was pregnant, he thought of her womb as a camera, the captured seed was a slide and cells multiplied an image into view. When the baby was born they named him Jacques, and were you to hold his skin up to the sun you would see a series of slides:

An infant nursing on a rocking chair.

A barefoot child catching frogs.

A boy floating on his back in a pond and clouds racing their reflections over him.

A teenager standing in the silence of a snowy wood.

And so on and on. Each image, each slide, a single molecule building the picture of Jacques and Mathis was there and he wasn't there, like light through the trees, the presence of Mathis was dappled.

*

When Jacques was younger his father carved him a large ark. It became a tradition to sit at the table with an encyclopedia and choose the animals for Mathis to whittle while he was away on expedition. One evening they came across a map of the American state of Illinois and there at the bottom, beside the Mississippi, was a town named Callisto.

"There's a town named after your bear," said Jacques.

"The Mississippi is a river I would love to see," said Mathis.

They made a plan to visit one day. His father outlined the state with his pen and stared at the map for a long time, then got up to make a cup of tea, while Jacques flipped through the pages searching for an animal his ark didn't already possess. A section about India had a photograph of a peacock with his tail spread. Jacques knew his father would be able to carve the patterns on the feathers perfectly.

"Their feathers look like eyes," said Jacques as he turned the book around for his father to see.

"Peacocks it is then," his father said and placed his hand on Jacques shoulder. "If I don't make it to Callisto, you go. There is no such thing in this world as a coincidence," he said, then sat by the fire and drank his tea.

That night his father's sleep had little growls inside it and Jacques knew he'd leave the following day. He always left during his black soil dreams and usually returned with the first snow.

Nora would run to him and pounce on him like a puppy. He'd laugh and stand there, letting her empty his pockets of presents, glossy feathers and stones with pictures on them. The snowflakes were penny sized and landed on their sweaters in patterns and melted. They would enter the warm house. Their discarded boots left puddles full of firelight. Mathis would reach inside his pack and give Jacques his whittled animals, then sit in his chair and speak for the first time in weeks.

The carvings were enhanced by his narrative. Jacques and his mother would draw up their knees under blankets, listen and drink tea. Magnificent, faraway sentences flew from his mouth like feathers dislodged from the hunt. It entranced them and the carvings were dry talismans they spun inside their hot hands. He told his stories beautifully. He did not speak of Callisto, yet she was there, within the shadows that flicked against the wall, like black flags, as they sat inside the half said.

*

The light in Canada was completely different to the light in Provence. It was not supple and affectionate and wheaten. It was arresting and sharp or nothing, and how an artist used this light deserved, demanded even, a certain level of stateliness that bears naturally cultivated.

The photographer is his light.

The photograph achieves an immortality that is familiar because the picture is both real and unreal. As soon as time is fixed, it's gone, but the photograph remembers and throws out a tentacle of recognition that's entirely personal to the viewer. It's this familiarity that haunts us, like a ghost in a dress we've secretly worn before.

The key word is secret. It was always an act of love. That was never a question. Years passed, and Mathis's photographs improved, because his secrets grew to the point where his obsession was almost revealed. Almost. The Almost kept it spiritual, kept it art. If Mathis's pictures were able to whisper they would undoubtedly speak of transformation.

For what becomes of a man who becomes his own beast?

What becomes of a man that doesn't?

3.

That summer Mathis came home early, but he was not himself, there were no rocks or feathers in his pockets, and he spent most of his time in his darkroom.

It was the summer of bluebottles.

Jacques remembers walking down the stairs in his pajamas. The room smelt of vinegar, lemon and unwashed hair. His mother was scrubbing tiny black spots from the woodwork with a wire brush and had already taken large circles of paint off the walls. Her actions were becoming increasingly manic, though this word did not factor into his vocabulary and he saw her as possessed. Her peach housecoat was hanging half open and covered in white paint flecks. Her feet and knees were filthy and stray strands of hair kinked like black spider legs from her messy braid. Her arms stopped moving when she heard him, and water dripped from her elbows into a puddle on the floor.

"It's as if we've been cursed," she said.

He let the comment hang in the room like an unheeded warning. What was there to say? He blinked at her. She was right. He went and made a cup of tea.

The summer heat had produced a plague of black flies. Bluebottles created a hive of iridescence between the storm windows and the house felt as though it was floating inside a crawling sea.

When the flies first arrived, Jacques helped his father remove the outer windows. The morning was yellow, hot and still. Their valley was scorched bland and the mountains rose like stone omens. The flies burst forward and landed a shiny glove on Jacques's face. He gagged and swallowed one by accident. His father pointed up to the black ribbon twisting out of view, and his mother, on the porch, began a round of applause. Mathis and Jacques joined her, and a row of pines that pitch-forked the sky caught the sound of their clapping as it skipped across the field. The sun had made them dizzy. Inside the house, Jacques drank a glass of water to dislodge the wing he had caught in his throat.

Of course, it had been useless, as the flies returned in droves, and like an organized army, they left black spots, smears and swirls on the woodwork and in corners. They bit and drew blood, and when they died, they left their flaky carcasses inside the thick orange carpeting. Their tiny black bodies crumbled under Jacques's bare feet. All summer long he picked wings and antennae out from between his toes.

*

Jacques pulled a chair up to the window and drank his tea. A fly squeezed through a small hole of broken sealant at the bottom of the window frame and whined with freedom. He put his tea down and waited. It landed and protracted its arms like windshield blades. He placed his thumb on top of it until he felt a pop, then walked to the back door and flicked its body towards the dry ground. It scattered with the others like blue-black scabs on a head of sedge grass.

Beyond the field, his father's boat rolled to shore. He had been fishing, and Jacques had heard him leaving at dawn, heard his zipper, his heels in boots, the turning doorknob, and then the peaceful nothingness of a person who has left. The window was a patch of chilly lavender and shadow, and he fell back to sleep curled under his warm quilt.

Jacques walked down to the pier. The fish hung from a tree like a line of silver darts. His father reached up, cut the line and threw them on the ground where they flapped droplets of musky water against Jacques's legs. His mother, dressed and composed once more, stomped down the hill drying a knife on her apron. Her hair was secured with clips. She did not look at Jacques. Instead, she looked at the fish and whistled her approval. Mathis smiled.

Jacques squatted next to his mother and helped her unhook the fish mouths. She chopped the heads off the smaller fish and gutted the rest. She gave him a newspaper full of entrails and fish heads.

"Bury it," she said and grabbed his arm.

His father was walking back to his boat.

"You hear me? Not a word. Bury it," she squeezed his arm and didn't blink.

He knew she wasn't talking about fish guts. He thought of her in her peach housecoat. He pushed her hand off his arm and she softened, recoiled.

"I'm so sorry. I'm so sorry, squirrel. I'm just tired, that's all," she said as she lifted her face towards the sun.

"I know," said Jacques.

She looked at him. Her eyes glistened like two bluebottles and infected everything, then she walked away.

A flock of geese flew overhead, noisy as a crowd of bicycle horns and he watched them land on the lake. It was incredibly still and the geese smeared across its reflected mountains like raindrops across a canvas. There was disruption all around him. He buried the fish guts in the garden and walked back to the house.

His mother was in the kitchen chopping onions. There were tears streaming down her face, so she hadn't noticed the onions turning pink.

"You're bleeding!" Jacques said.

She stopped, dried her eyes on her sleeve and looked down with amazement at the cut between her thumb and forefinger. It was long and deep. She dipped her finger in the pool of blood, licked it and grabbed a tea towel. The blood mushroomed through the cloth like a red cloud.

"It's nothing. Here," she gave him the knife and swatted flies as she ran down the hallway. He finished chopping the onions.

He knew she hadn't felt a thing.

4.

There were other clues. Once she dropped a spoonful of chili on the floor and when she couldn't pick it up, began banging her hand against the wall. His father had been away on expedition and by the time he returned, the bruise was a pale yellow as if someone had rubbed a dandelion across her knuckles.

After his eyes adjusted to it, he saw it everywhere.

To him the word illness meant stomach bug or cough. It meant hot soup, not sudden outbursts of vowels like loud, frustrated claps. It meant blankets, not dead hands. Her hands were the first to lose their feeling. They were battered, bruised and cut. He knew when she could feel because she'd ask him to sit next to her, then she'd run her hands up and down his arms, his chest, stopping to feel his heart beat, through his hair and then softly, softly across his face and cheeks.

By the end of the summer her arms were thin as a child's. They were ropes she wrapped around herself as if trying to hold together the pieces of a shipwreck. In her eyes she carried the same mysteriousness of the sea and could not be helped or predicted or guided. Her illness was like a superstition his father refused to talk about. The problem was that his father was not a seafaring man. He was a woodsman. He knew wood and very little of water. He was not prepared to learn something new. Sometimes it is simply the refusal of change that initiates change so suddenly.

*

Nora was pouring boiled blackberries into pint jars for jam. It was late summer. The black braid hanging between her shoulder blades began to twitch as she took quick glimpses behind her. Jacques was seated at the table removing sticks and leaves from the final bowl of blackberries, and his father was across from him marking a map with a pencil. He was the first to notice her twitching. He put his pencil down and nodded at Jacques. She was shaking. Suddenly she turned around, still holding the hot pot and splashing boiling blackberry juice over her arms and bare feet. She dropped the pot, scurried a little on the juice and backed away from them as if she didn't recognize who they were. She looked like a scared animal.

"Nora?" his father said. "Norabird, what's wrong?"

He got up and started walking towards her, but she crouched away from him and held her hands in front of her face. She was mumbling something over and over again. There was a rancid burning smell.

"Her hair!" Jacques pointed at Nora's head.

Her braid was alight with flames. Mathis lunged towards her, but she kicked him away, and started dashing back and forth across the kitchen floor. Her arms were flailing. The jars of blackberry juice crashed to the floor. His father slipped and slid while trying to chase her, finally he caught her.

"The sink!" Jacques shouted.

His father thrust Nora's head into the sink. She was clawing and scratching his arms. When he brought her back up she gulped for air, then slapped him, hard, across the face. Her eyes were back. She was back with them. Her scream was wet.

"Your hair was on fire," he rubbed the red handprint on his cheek. "I had to."

"What?" she reached behind her and winced when she felt her burnt scalp.

She looked around the room. There was broken glass and blackberry juice everywhere. Their feet were bleeding. She let out a small whimper.

"Come on," his father said, while gently taking her by the arm, "let's have a look."

It was a sticky limp across the floor. He sat her in a chair and stood above her with his eyes closed, then took a deep breath, and looked at her scalp. He breathed a sigh of relief.

"They're only surface burns. You'll be sore for a while, but it's nothing to worry about. You'll be just fine. Though we'll have to trim the rest of your hair Nora. I'll just do that now okay?"

He asked Jacques to make a paste of baking soda and water while he went to get the scissors and bandages. She sat in the chair, completely bewildered, and stared at her hands.

"There's glass in them," she said.

"Yes, you had an accident," his father told her, "I'll take care of that in a moment, just as soon as I finish fitting this bandage. There. A few weeks and you'll be as good as new. Now let me see those hands. Right, Jacques can you fetch me the tweezers?"

He removed large, angry shards of glass from her hands and her feet. She didn't flinch. He did the same to himself and cursed bitterly under his breath.

"I don't understand," she muttered while Mathis led her to bed.

Jacques cleaned up the mess and sat down at the table. He looked at the map of British Columbia his father had been marking and read Callisto, Callisto, Callisto all along the mountains like a love drawing or a mantra.

*

It was the risk that made Mathis feel alive, the risk of losing, not his life, but the intensity of the moment by coming one step too close. He began to crave the adrenaline that stretched like a tripwire between himself and Callisto. The camera was a way to trap that vertigo through explosion, flash, in a box that he could take apart with his hands. If he could, he would have taken himself apart. He would have reassembled himself. It was violent like that. It was violent in the way that making love is violent, for what is essential for our survival, can also drive us beyond our own control. He could not control himself or his desires any more than he could control Callisto. But. He could house the two of them inside a slide, so that he owned his weakness, and like a magician, he could revive them from darkness and into the focus of light.

*

Jacques and his father were collecting firewood.

"I notice you haven't been carving," his father said.

It was true. Resurrecting the mouse had scared Jacques and he'd been afraid to carve since. What if it happened again, or worse yet, what if it didn't? It had felt so natural that Jacques now wondered if it had actually happened at all. His father moved a log and made a satisfied grunt.

"Look here," he said and pointed to the ground.

It was a small thing. A seashell deep inside the capacious lungs of the forest like a perfect pink cyst. His father picked it up.

"It happens sometimes that an echo of the past can make its way to the surface. The seabed that produced the shell a million years before the forest grew proves the soil's legacy, but the forest cannot remember anything beyond its own existence and has no recollection of the watery beginnings it feeds from. We live inside our enclosures," he said, "and occasionally, we wake up inside the wrong one. Your maman, my mother, was Creole and would be upset with me for saying that. There are no wrong enclosures, she'd say, the soul learns what it needs to know for its entire journey. She was a guide. A translator of enclosures. Some people thought she was crazy. Others thought she was wise. Crazy or wise, my photographs guide me, soothe me, and she taught me that there is no other way to live. I want to tell you this," Mathis placed the shell inside of Jacques's hand. "When you find your essence, be true to it. If you are a shell that wakes inside a forest, do not deny the ocean, guide it towards you. Guiding is a part of your legacy. There are the fossils of your maman inside of you."

The shell in the forest, thought Jacques as he looked at his father, the bear in the skin. The creator within.

The starling arrived the next day. It has been killed for sport by one of the cats and left beside the front door as a present. Jacques picked it up and inspected the two clean little holes inside its chest. What if it had fledglings? A power is not corrupting if it's used for good, he thought, and carried the bird upstairs.

*

As his ability to resurrect small animals matured, it was as though the forest knew, so brought to him it's recently perished. He built a long shelf above his bed and placed all of his resurrections on top of it. There were lots of mice and birds, a few rabbits and a single glorious vixen. He had found her by a stream. Her coat was wet and solid with frost. He didn't have a piece of wood with him that was fox sized, so decided to try with the small bit of maple he had in his satchel. He sat down beside her and began to carve and pray. The water gently rocked her beautiful, russet form, from her white throat hung miniature icicles. He thought of how he would use a hot poker from the fire and gently singe her forelegs and the tips of her ears black. When she was awakened, he'd locate the black flecks in her eyes.

She did not run away from him like the others had, but stretched her limbs and took a drink of water, before looking directly at him and walking into the wood. For a moment, Jacques wondered if she might speak to him, so abundant was her spirit, and he felt their organisms align. The vixen reminded him of how his maman would have been, a majestic survivalist, a mystery outside of the mind's field.

When you understand this, when you begin to live outside of your enclosure, it is not inconceivable that the essence of one thing might fall into another. That a vixen might resemble his maman, that lives should link, though this was never the physical case with Jacques. His arms were arms, not wings, his hands were hands, not claws, but through them he could raise the shells from the soil. In resurrecting he never produced the entire personality, rather the substance that was the strongest, so when his mother began to lose her mind, he carved and carved her hands, for they had always been the strongest.

*

A pair of loons called out inside the crickets' hum. Jacques put down his book and went to the open window. His mother was sleeping. The sun was sinking and Jacques could see Mathis rolling a large log from the woodland. A trail of bulldozed grass stretched all the way to his darkroom. When Mathis reached the door he turned it upright and wrapped his arms around it with his face against the bark. It looked as though he were wrestling someone. Jacques heard the log thunk in the corner.

Jacques left the house and followed the trail of bent grass to the edge of the woods. The forest floor was springy, covered with pine needles and mossy stumps like half-hidden trolls.

Mosquitoes shrilled through the ferns and spiny thicket, a few owls piccoloed off the dense alders, where small funnels of evening lit up the occasional tree, but otherwise the canopy was evergreen thick. One of these funnels spotlighted a split tree trunk that sat in the ground like a shard of glass.

It reminded him of his mother's hands.

It was an old wound and leg-thick branches lay on the ground. It was beautiful wood, soft and easy to manipulate. Jacques picked up as much as he could carry and walked back to the house. It was almost dark and orange holes were glowing from his father's darkroom. Jacques piled the wood on the porch and squat down to choose a piece to carve. It was smooth, unknotted and the size of a forearm.

He let his knife decide the shape the wood would take. The forms he was carving at that time transcended classification, like a sigh or laughter transcends language. He drilled small holes in the bottom of each sculpture and stuck them on a stick fixed inside a block of wood.

He thought of them as sensations. His mother called them shrunken heads. He placed them in his bedroom window, where their shadows cast strange boulder shapes across the floor. He liked the view between them. Sometimes he carved a certain shape purely to break the view, to crack the space around it, and rift the surge of atoms like a bubble in a life that's sedimenting.

He was learning to carve himself, to thumbprint and convert the wood into his own creation. He looked down at his carving and saw that it was becoming another small, cupped hand, and imagined removing his mother's hands at the wrist and replacing them with ones of his own making. They would be beautifully carved with stars for knuckles and diamonds for fingernails.

5.

Mathis's darkroom was a shed without windows that sat twenty paces from the house. Each wall had three fist-sized holes for ventilation and when Mathis was developing his photographs, he nailed a flat board over the holes. It had been days since Mathis had left his darkroom, yet the holes remained uncovered. Through them, Jacques could see small movements of light, shadow, and once, even an arch of piss. Mathis ate carrots, string beans, rolled-up bread, anything that would fit through the holes. He refused to open the door.

When Jacques told his mother that he was worried about his Father she said, "I'm not. I'm beyond it. I'm beyond caring about what happens inside his love shed. You don't see me in there, do you?"

It was true. Nobody was allowed to look inside. If Mathis needed something he pushed his lips through the wall like a slug and shouted. Jacques passed him screwdrivers, long sticks, tacks and wildflowers. Jacques saw photographs glossing the walls and a thick silhouette in the corner. He wondered if it was the log he'd seen his father rolling and squinted towards the figure.

"Take your eyes off her. You have no business looking at her," his father said.

His eye floated like a knot in the wood.

*

Mathis had been inside his darkroom for five days when Nora started throwing things at the wall. The objects she threw grew twice their size in the long autumn light and hit the wall like monsters.

Jacques took the knives and scissors from the kitchen drawer, threw them in a bag and left. She didn't notice. She was caught in a rhythm. He walked past his father's darkroom, three holes flickered with gaslight, and all the way to the lake.

He sat cross-legged on the dock. The reflection of a few stars lay trapped in the lake like fireflies in a black jar. Nude fish mouths wrinkled the water's skin. He took his knife and a small, unfinished carving from his pocket. It was a pawn. The last piece to his set. He and his father played chess during the winter when the bears were hibernating. The sky was as dark as it would get on a full moon and behind him the house anchored like a bright ship.

The lake held even the Milky Way.

At its bottom the fish slept with stars on their backs.

He thought about this. He thought about the burn of possibility.

He walked back to the house. His father was still in his darkroom, softly singing. Cold air rushed him through the door. She wasn't asleep, instead, sat in a pile of torn clothes and didn't look up.

"You're too hard on things," she said, mending one of his shirts.

The needle stabbed her thumb. The stitching was large and irregular. On the table he could see little pinprick indentions scattered across the surface like beads. Mathis opened the door and Jacques hardly recognized him. His face was smeared and hairy. There were many things different about him, but the most noticeable was the smell.

"Look at how useful I am," Nora said holding up a crudely darned shirt. "Aren't I useful?"

*

The first snow came and lasted for days. It drifted ground level with the windows ledge and cast a strange bleaching light into the house. Mathis began digging a path to the woodpile. The shovel scraped inside silence. Outside there was a crow. Inside, Nora slept in a puddle of sweat and moved in and out of consciousness. Jacques made a venison pie for dinner and listened to a mouse nesting in the roof.

Mathis turned his face towards the mountain. It was always snowing on the mountaintop, and if Mathis had remained on the mountain for too long, he could begin to feel as though he were drowning in the white glare. His eyes would start to search for structure and color, an edge, a deepening in the path and that's when he knows that it's time to leave. He often drank the sight of the first flower he'd come across poking like a beautiful hand through the snow, his descent into the green valley could melt him with its suppleness. He knew there was no thirst like the thirst for the green and living world.

He thought about this as he stacked a wall of wood behind the stove. He wanted to say something meaningful to Jacques who was reading at the table. The smell of cooking venison filled the room, and Jacques could feel the cold from his father's body as he stood above him. There seemed to be no way to undo what had been done. He closed his book and looked up at his father in his overcoat and work gloves.

"She's stuck on the mountain," Mathis said. "But you're not."

It explained everything and nothing at the same time.

"I'll only be away for a little while."

"Don't," Jacques implored.

"I promise I'll come back."

6.

In the morning Mathis was gone. Jacques woke to a cold house, dressed and went to stoke the fire. He placed the kettle on top of the stove, put on his boots and damp coat and went outside to replenish the wood basket. He didn't want to touch the wall of wood his father had built.

As soon as he opened the door his moisture instantly froze. His breath hung in front of his face in little exhales of fog. Above him, stars like lighthouses filled the morning sky. He walked to the logs stacked alongside the house. The black tarp that covered them had frozen to the wood, and when he jerked it free, he ripped off the top layer of bark. The logs were icy and smooth in his bare hands as he threw them into the basket.

Birdsong took the sharpness out of the air. He could hear his mother coughing upstairs. The kitchen was warm when he returned and the kettle was boiling. He put the full basket next to the stove and made two cups of tea.

Months passed and blizzards came and went.

His mother slept through it all in her sweat. Her breath rose and fell with effort. It snagged on every gurgle. Jacques melted snow on the stove and spoon-fed her. Their larder was nearly empty and everything fresh had long been devoured. In the evenings he read or whittled or did anything to avoid confronting the inevitable. The piano beside the sofa beckoned him with its promise of irregular noise. He didn't want to wake her. Sometimes he put the lid down and played intense, inaudible songs.

Time was both fast and slow.

Then, one evening, he found himself standing at the door to his father's darkroom. Hibernation was close to death, he thought, perhaps he could carve Callisto and bring his father to him. A key on a string dangled from his gloved hand.

Jacques had nearly stopped believing his father would return. It seemed like their only chance. The sound of his boots crunching in the snow and the owls echoed in his lonely chest. His heart was beating fast. His mother had stopped eating all together. It wouldn't be long. She was mumbling in her sleep when he left the house.

He needed the strength, however forbidden, that his father seemed to find inside this room. He was desperate. He looked up at the moon, white stone cut by black branches. He opened the door and stepped inside.

It was black and smelled feral. He switched on his flashlight. It shone a yellow spot on the floor while his eyes adjusted. He was afraid to look at the walls. He was afraid, but did it anyway and what he saw repulsed and fascinated him.

They were covered with pictures of Callisto. The pictures were framed with some kind of mud. He smelt it. It was bear feces. Inside the scat his father had placed little stones and twigs in interwoven patterns. Feathers and bits of flower were delicately pressed into his finger swirls. It was disturbingly beautiful.

He saw her in the corner.

He shined his flashlight on the carved image of Callisto, but she wasn't exactly a bear. Her face was more human than bear. Her paws were human hands. She was serene, almost perfect and adorned with wreaths of withered wildflowers. Large clumps of fur were glued to her body. Her eyes seemed to plead for release. There was a cough behind him, he turned and found his mother standing just beyond the door, clutching her nightdress to her throat.

"You shouldn't have done that," she said. Her voice was a whisper.

She was barefoot in the snow. Her frail body quivered underneath her nightdress and her eyes were wide and wild. She looked like a ghost.

"You scared me. What are you doing out here, it's freezing, you'll catch cold. Come on. Come back inside," he said, but she just stared at him.

"You shouldn't have done that," she said again.

"Done what?"

"Gone inside," she nodded towards the shed.

"I was just locking it up," he said.

She was beginning to scare him. Her voice was incredibly flat, but her face was hateful.

"Liar! Now he'll smell you and never come back!" she shouted and lunged towards him.

Her teeth were bluish white in the moonlight. Her fingernails dug into his neck. He tried to push her off, he didn't want to fight her, he kept shouting at her to stop, but she was vicious. She clung and bit. Her body, her skin was hot and jagged. He couldn't believe her strength, her bones were sharp and powerful and her face was a scream. She was tearing out his hair when he seized her hand. Her mouth attacked his glove and she bit and spat until she reached his skin. He smacked her and she fell back into the bloodied snow. She was spitting with exhaustion.

She let him pick her up and carry her back into the house. She was shivering by the time he put her in bed. He pulled the blankets up to her chin, she said nothing and closed her eyes. He fetched another blanket from his bed to wrap around her shaking body. When he returned he saw that her head had fallen off the pillow. He gently placed his hand behind her neck and lifted. She was unconscious and limp, but alive. He knew she couldn't stay alive for long. He wanted it finished and complete, so leant down to her ear and whispered.

"Don't be afraid. I'll bring you back," then softly placed the pillow over her face and pressed.

She gave one small lurch before she went still. It was appallingly peaceful.

7

He couldn't stay; there wasn't enough food, yet he couldn't leave her there. What if his father came back and found her? So he collected her body and walked to the door. Outside the world was quiet, but for his footprints and the crystalline clouds of his staggered breathing. Wisps against a starry sky. He knew what he had to do.

He walked slowly towards the ravine.

It was deep and hidden and he threw her down it like a stick. Her nightdress billowed before she began to descend. There had been nothing left of her, he consoled himself. Heavy flakes of snow added another layer of silent insulation. There was no sound. No wind. No mice, owls or fox. His animal had left as well. His animal was at the bottom of the ravine.

Now he needed noise. He clapped his hands. He leapt up and ran aimlessly in circles, shouting, screaming and kicking snow into the air, until he collapsed and rolled himself into a ball. The snow melted around his heat. It cooled his forehead.

He was wet and tired, so tired. Inside the house looked warm and golden. There were parts of himself he could not feel. He rose and walked towards the door. He closed the door behind him and locked it.

He lay down by the fire and fell asleep.

Her eyes filled his dreams.

All night, her body slowly disappeared beneath a skin of snow, his dreams. He slept the following day. The next evening he entered the woods. The pines were black. The birch trees appeared to be made of silver moon skin. It made him look at his own hands, ungloved in the freezing air, chapped, stark and, he now realized, capable of death as well as rebirth, life. She had died in his hands. He had held her head like a large frozen egg. He shook her a little, just to be sure, as though death were something one could crack out of, as though she might rattle a clue.

*

The morning sky was white and startling and he stood underneath it alone. It did not feel heavy. He couldn't stay in Pine Creek. But what if his father came back? It was possible that he was just stranded at a post in the mountains and would return in the spring. Anything was possible.

He thought of the town Callisto.

It seemed like a way to be close and far away. He craved an expedition, a place where he could sculpt in peace and learn to develop his gift of resurrection. A place where he could bring his mother back, healthy and sane.

He walked inside and took the encyclopedia down from the shelf. He sat on the floor in a square of cold sun, the animals shone on the pages, and when he reached the Mississippi, he stopped. She was vein blue and Callisto, Illinois was attached to her like a cyst, like a knot, like a fist.

*

It is easy to get a passport when you have money and are the grandson of a French General. Over the next month, he reported his mother missing and bought a house in Callisto, near the river, north of town and out of the way. He shipped his books, his tools, a few sculptures, his father's photography and his French cutlery.

The night before he left, he took his carvings from the shelves and held them one by one. He opened the encyclopedia to Illinois, placed it on the table and stood his carvings around it in a circle. On the page he wrote, *I am here*, just in case his father returned, but also because he wanted to preserve the moment he began living his own life. He imagined dust coating the page and the Mississippi like a fine ice. Soon birds will nest and splat Illinois with their tiny white meteor explosions.

In the morning, he carried a single bag to the train.

It was as loud as a tunneling dream. It had silver bones, bolted joints, grilled teeth and a black face, he stepped inside its snarl, and clicked open a glass eye to breathe. Only the icicles near the steam dripped on the platform.

The mountains were ripped charcoal drawings pasted to a blue sheet and as the train left, they began to smudge. He moved his thumb along the dark pines that bearded their bases. Enormous black lakes, like oceans, mirrored beside him. He was the only passenger in the compartment and could let himself think aloud, could let his mouth hang open as he stared at the racing. When night fell he saw a single light ahead. A station, he thought, or America, whatever it is, I'm heading straight towards it like a ferocious black moth. He opened his arms like wings.

*

All the way there he imagined he was sitting by the riverbank of the Mississippi. Skips of gold were on the swells. The sun was hot and the sorrow in him gagged like a sheath he'd swallowed. When I'm ready, he thought, I'll begin pulling it from my ears, my eyes, my nose and it will slip from my fingers and land on the water like a gray scum, it will float downriver, it will break as it slams against the ocean, it will break and dissolve and I'll never see it again. Then I'll be empty and free for the wind to inhabit, he thought, he dreamed, the wind.

8.

Callisto, Illinois

The walk from the station took him half a day. It was a different country's heat. He followed the map, stayed close to the river and didn't see another human soul. But there was sun everywhere, warm and penetrating and the sky was a lonely heartbreaking blue, and it occurred to him that the clearest view of a place was from a distance.

Already, Pine Creek seemed like a life away, another life that belonged to someone that resembled him. He had begun to think of himself as a person he was about to meet.

The house he had bought had two identities as well.

From its west side stretched a flat green palm of prairie; a runway for the wind that whipped with paint-tearing force and left bits of timber bare and exposed like gray sores on a body. Its east side gently sloped to the river. It reminded Jacques of an old clown who'd applied only half of his white makeup.

Both sides of the house produced waves, the grass and the water flowed together, so that it was immersed in constant movement, like an island one could walk to. A single track arrowed through grasses and into town, Jacques stood on it, and grasshoppers stuck to his legs.

The key was in the mailbox. He opened the door and stood on the threshold. A cobweb stuck to his face. The windows were without curtains and sunlight slanted across the floor in a way that seemed cathedral-like and pious.

"Pity you haven't got a bride to carry in," said a voice behind him.

He jumped and turned around. It was an old and wrinkled woman with white hair that stood on her head like a dandelion clock. She wore binoculars around her neck, high waist jeans rolled halfway up her calves and men's shoes. She laughed with all of her teeth.

"You can use my ol' bag of bones if you want, that don't mean we have to consummate anything, mind you, unless ..." she winked at him. He must have looked as shocked as he felt.

"Oh Jesus, sorry," she laughed. "I'm sorry. I shouldn't be frisky until I've properly introduced myself. I didn't mean to scare ya. I'm just being nosey, that's all. Came to check out my new neighbor. How do you do? Names Birdie Dubois," she said and stuck out her hand.

"Nice to meet you Mrs. Dubois. I'm Jacques Beaumont," he said and took her hand in his.

"It's Miss. Always Miss. I like it that way. Well, here you go," she shoved a lump of tin foil against his chest.

"What's this?"

"Banana bread. It's a welcome gift but don't get too excited, I'm a terrible baker."

"Oh. Well, thank you anyway," he said.

She nodded and smiled.

"So are you going to invite me in or do I have to make up some excuse about incontinence?"

"No, no come in, sorry, I, well I'm not used to visitors. I don't even know where the bathroom is anyway."

"I do. Right over there," she pointed to a half open door. "My God this is a rat trap. What the hell did you buy it for?"

He was unable to answer. She was right. The house hadn't been lived in for some time. Why did he buy it? To remake all that he'd lost, he thought, to grieve and sculpt, to become anew.

"I'm not sure. I wanted to be alone. Actually, I am alone. I guess I'm waiting to find out why I bought it, why I'm here, if that makes any sense," he said.

"Honest answers seldom make sense," she looked around with her hands on her hips. "At least the windows are still intact. And, good Lord, is that what I think it is?" Birdie pointed to a large object covered with a sheet in the corner.

Jacques walked over and pulled the sheet away with a puff of dust. Mouse droppings flung across the floor like hen seed. It was a grand piano.

"I don't believe it! They left their piano!" Birdie walked up to it and traced a big B in the dust.

Her fingertip was wet black and she wiped it across her jeans like paint.

"Who's 'They'?"

"The Zimmermans," she said and struck a chord and the piano was badly out of tune. "Yikes. The Zimmermans, you know, the people who used to live here. Oh, the parties we had back when I was totally gorgeous and kissed all the men, and women for that matter, with my tongue. I can't believe they left their piano. I could tune it for you? Can you play?"

"Yes, actually, I can. My mother taught me. But I'm not really sure I should keep it."

"What? Why?"

"Because it must belong to somebody right? It feels strange having it here."

"Listen. Anyone who'd give a hoot about this piano is dead or livin' with dementia in the dustbowl. You keep it. Better welcome gift then my banana bread and believe me this house could use a bit of levity, I know it. I feel it, I feel things."

She looked though the binoculars she had hanging around her neck.

"Here comes Jimmy The Mail Man. He's an ass, but it's tolerable because he's always on time. I'll be back tomorrow with a dustpan and a mop," she said as she walked down the porch steps and towards the river.

"Thanks again for the bread," he called after her and she waved without turning around.

The house was incredibly quiet after she left. She was like a mini tornado. He unwrapped the bread, broke off a bit, put it in his mouth and spat it out again. It tasted like salt and detergent. Detergent. He could use some detergent. He was ripe with sweat. Jimmy knocked on the door. After this, he thought, I will bathe and sleep. When he opened the door Jimmy was obviously shocked.

"Who are you?" Jimmy asked and Jacques felt a punch of confrontation. Birdie hadn't been wrong.

"Jacques Beaumont. Who are you?"

"*You're* Jacques Beaumont?"

"Yes. Is that a problem?"

"Nope. Just a surprise is all. We thought you was French."

"I am," Jacques said and Jimmy laughed.

"No you ain't. Look. I got your stuff in back, five boxes right?"

"That's right. Let me give you a hand."

"I reckon you can manage," he said as he opened the rear door to his van.

Jacques carried each box to the porch while Jimmy sat in his van. His arm hung out the window, bent like a tanned chicken wing. The skin above his shirtsleeve was white.

Jacques unloaded the five boxes and placed them in the corner of the living room. He opened one and took out his blanket and pillow. Upstairs he chose the smallest room because it had the best view of the river. A path as straight as a seam plowed its way to the water's edge. He lay down on the floor and fell asleep. He dreamt he was walking along the path and the ground behind him was unfastening.

*

That man's an Accidental if ever there was one, thought Birdie. She had a bird for everybody and he was a bird spotted outside of his territory, that was for sure. The walk home from Jacques had been satisfying. She had seen an Indigo Bunting on a yellow maple and felt grateful, as she did every day, for her eyesight. Take my knees, she often thought, but leave my eyes and a window. She walked inside her house, threw her binoculars on the sofa and went to pour herself a glass of lemonade.

Franklin, her parrot, was in the kitchen.

"Franklin, you'll never guess, but I spotted myself a human Accidental this afternoon," she said and put her feet up on the kitchen table.

"Accidental," said Franklin.

"Yep, you bet your green feathered ass. When I saw him I said to myself two things: O Lord he's black and O Lord help him. Nobody expected a black man. The rumor was he was a Frenchman, but, of course, when you get to thinking about it, Frenchmen can be black too, obviously. He's an outcast, and I gotta tell ya, I liked him immediately. Jacques Beaumont. Mr. Class and Manners. He pronounced my name properly with an accent Franklin. Dubois."

"Dubois," said Franklin.

"That's right my darlin' like opening your mouth for the dentist, ahhhh, not Oi Sea, like the frigging potato state. I don't even like potatoes. And he's a handsome son of a bitch, oh boy, if I was younger I'd have had him in the hay. Do your rolling now before your back plays up, that's my advice," she said to no one in particular.

"He has skin as smooth as a horse's neck. Honestly, you've never seen a man, a young man, mind you, a kid really, so out of place. That face for a start. Two cheekbones wide and smooth as the rounded ridge of a buckeye. That color too, a deep, deep brown. His nose fills the space between his wide set eyes. Kinda like an ox on hind legs, you know, handsome in an irregular, interesting way. There's not a dent or a dimple on him. He looks like he was born serious. A serious mystery, no doubt. I tell you he's running from something. He stinks of hidden places. Nobody comes here out of the blue, Franklin, nobody. It's just not a place you stumble upon. You got to have relations or a secret, and Lord knows he's not related to anybody around here. I hope they just leave him be, but I doubt it. I'm worried about him, Franklin."

"Worried," said Franklin.

"Me too."

9

Birdie arrived the following morning as promised. She brought a ladder, some cleaning supplies and a Sears catalogue. The phone was working, so Jacques ordered a bed, a refrigerator and a few other essentials, while Birdie polished and tuned the piano.

She took a small bundle of sage from her bag, lit it until it was smoking, and then walked around each room muttering a low chant. Jacques cleaned the windows and removed a bird's nest from the oven.

"I'm going to light a fire with the rest of this," she waved the sage in the air. "Just to clear your flue."

Jacques nodded yes. He was cleaning the baseboards and layers of dust came off like fur. He thought of Callisto and his mother and walked outside to collect some kindling. The land was bone dry, but he could sense fertility underneath the dirt.

"We're in a drought now," Birdie had told him, "but usually this soil is so fertile you can bury spit in the ground and a mouth will rise up singing, yep, it turns veins into roots overnight."

He thought about green blood. He took a deep breath and felt dirt clinging to his nostrils. Everything was subdued by a hot fume, the sky, the ground, the glare encasing the trees, the rolling glare on the river. The colors here did not come in big blocks, but as flashes, orange on a pheasant's wing, the rush of a red wing, pink smears in the clouds.

Back home in the mountains, the snow would still be blanketing his mother. He didn't feel like thinking. He walked to the side of the river. The water slapped like syrup against the bank. He could even hear this swishing from his bedroom window. It was everywhere. He plugged his ears and heard his own heart swish, his black reflection on the water, behind his eyes, waiting for him.

There was nothing he could have done. He unplugged his ears and the tall grass hissed with insects. The sound was a kind of radiance, a drum, and he listened to it until his mother disappeared.

Boxelder bugs clung to the screen door and dropped like black and orange peas when he slammed it shut. The floors glistened with Pine Sol. There were little bouquets of herbs in each of the corners and geodes were on every windowsill. Jacques handed Birdie the sticks he'd collected. She made a tent above the sage and struck a match.

"You ever seen a geode?" Birdie asked him.

"Is that what this is?" Jacques picked one up and glittered it in the sunlight.

"Yep. This area's covered with them. They look like normal rocks until you crack them open and find they are full of crystals. I've known a lot of people like that. It's only when you're broken open that your true self is revealed," she said. "You'll be fine, you know. It'll all be worth it, just wait, even if it takes a good long while, it'll be worth it all. Just be careful."

"I don't know what you mean," he said, a little startled that he'd been so transparent.

"I know you're running from something. You don't have to tell me what it is, but," Jacques stopped her.

"I'm here because my mother died," he said.

"I'm sorry to hear that," Birdie said.

"I needed to be somewhere else and the name Callisto means something to me."

"Callisto. Ursa Major. Now let me think. You part bear or something?" Birdie said and Jacques laughed.

"That's about right. Now, let me think. Are you part witch or something?" Jacques said and it was Birdie's turn to laugh.

"Touché," she said. "But seriously, this isn't Canada. You're a generation removed from Klan activities, so I mean it when I say, be careful."

"If it's so bad then why are you here?" He asked.

"I'm here because I was born here, plus, I'm needed," she said.

"By whom?"

"Everybody. Right now, you. Tomorrow, who knows?"

She threw her hands to heaven.

*

He was numb for days, too numb to dream, to create, to resurrect. He mended and painted the house. He planted a garden and ordered a shipment of logs. He went around touching things, stones, flowers, doorknobs and asking for forgiveness.

Birdie brought him groceries and he cooked and ate his meals in silence. He walked through the night until he was tired enough to sleep. It was as if his dreams wanted him alive before they'd enter him. They waited until he could feel again, until his awareness was sharpened by grief, each hair on his body like a small steel receptor ready to dig the dream in, so that when it arrived it stayed with him always, always the same dream:

He's watching a rabbit twitching in a field. A black dog jumps from the woods. It chases the rabbit around and around him in circles. He can't run away. He can't move. He looks down. Two mouths have swallowed his feet and are slowly chomping up his legs. The dog finally catches the rabbit and drops it at his side. He looks again. It's not the rabbit at all, but a hand with stars for knuckles, spit laced and gnawed.

10.

Arlo Donnelly sat in the window of Rosa's Café digesting the fried egg sandwich he'd just eaten for breakfast and drank the rest of his coffee. At 8:00am he wiped his mouth on a paper napkin, got up with a groan, put his Sheriff's hat on and walked across the street to CC's Grocery Store.

"Morning," said Calem Carson McKinney III. "Morning," replied Arlo.

CC's had been in the McKinney family for three generations and, for inheriting purposes, every boy in the McKinney family had to have the CC initials. CC's great-grandfather, Conway Cooper, began the store as an outpost when Callisto was a newly formed river town. Arlo grabbed a basket and stood beside Mrs. Johnson in the bread aisle.

"Lord CC, how many types of bread do you need?"

Arlo stood with his hands on his hips, making his belly look even bigger. His skin was the exact color of his beige uniform. His badge flashed like a silver nipple on his chest.

"Got to cater for all kinds these days," said CC.

"I'll say. Whole wheat? Who eats this crap?"

"You do. That's what Elora buys," said CC. Elora was Arlo's wife.

"No kiddin'? Well I'm getting white. I like white. Whole wheat's for Communist's," he said and CC laughed.

"How is Elora anyway?' CC said.

"Good, real good, apart from having the flu again and all, but, yeah, good," he said and flung the bread into his shopping cart.

"She must be sick. I never thought I'd see you doing women's business," said CC.

"Yeah, well. When needs must," he said, filling the cart with tins of baked beans. Hope, CC's daughter, noticed Arlo's knuckles were swollen. She looked at her father, but he avoided her gaze.

"Cheer up," CC smacked Arlo on the back. "She'll be jumping outta bed just as soon as she sees you only brought back beer, beans and white bread."

"She better be. Hey, speaking of Red's, you seen any sign of our new resident? Thought maybe he might've needed some milk by now."

"You mean the one who bought the ol' Zimmerman place?"

"That's right," said Arlo as he began to unload the groceries.

"Hope get over here and help this man. He can barely reach past his breakfast," CC laughed.

"Watch your mouth. I'll have you locked up," Arlo seemed relieved the subject had turned from Elora.

"Why? You think he's a Communist?" CC asked.

"Hell, I don't know, he's Canadian ain't he? And French. So I'm using my powers of estimation," Arlo said, took a mint from his shirt pocket and popped it in his mouth.

"Well, what I can't figure out is why on earth would he buy a place at the dog end of nowhere?" Mrs. Johnston said, who, until then, had been making a face-straining decision between a blue and a red dish towel. "Lord, the price of livin' these days," she added, looking at the price tags.

"That's a beautiful house," said Hope. She returned to the cash register and began ringing up Arlo's purchases.

"It's haunted," said Mrs. Johnston.

"Yeah, but in a peaceful way," said Hope and her father gave her a look that said, no backtalk young lady.

"Never mind that, it's next to that mad ol' bag Birdie. That woman wears men's work boots for Christ's sake. That witch would put the heebie-jeebies in me. Plus it ain't modern" said Arlo sucking his mint through his teeth while Hope bagged his groceries as well.

"No, but it's close to the river," said Hope.

"There's hardly a track that runs out there. What'll he do when the rain comes or the snow?" CC said.

"Oh yes, the snow, think of it," said Mrs. Johnston. She stood wringing her hands behind Arlo.

"Was a time when tracks weren't important if you were by the river, but river days are done, long gone since they built the highway, now a person needs a car and a reliable track."

"Oh yes, the highway. Harold services the car every year, I can't fault him," said Mrs. Johnston.

"Good man," Arlo said and CC hummed in agreement.

"But do you know what I heard?" Mrs. Johnston's voice was just above a whisper. "You'll never believe this. But. I heard he was an artist."

"An artist! See? What the hell'd I tell you? A damn Red! I'll ask Jimmy about him this afternoon," Arlo picked up his bag of groceries.

"No need to wait," said CC, standing by the window. "Mail van just pulled up outside the bank."

*

Jimmy was unloading some packages when Arlo tapped him on the shoulder.

"Hey Jimmy, you met our new friend yet?"

"Sure have," Jimmy said smirking so much that Arlo thought about smacking that smirk right off his face.

"Well, what's the verdict?" Arlo asked.

"You're not gonna believe this, but he's a black man."

"I hope to hell you're talking about intentions."

"No Sir. He's colored."

"Colored? What? Nancy told me his grandma was so French she needed a goddamn translator when she called up here, helped him buy the house and all. He's the grandson of a goddamn French General with a bank account to match and you're telling me he's a nigger?"

"Yes Sir."

"Well, shit, wonders never cease."

"What you gonna do?"

"Nothing but my oath and duty Jimmy. If he orders anything I wanna know about it."

"Oh, he's been ordering all kinds of stuff."

"Has he now, such as?"

"Such as a shipment of timber logs."

"What the hell does he need them for?"

"Gladys at the telephone office told me, that he told her, he was a wood carver of all things."

"Yeah I heard he was some sort of artist."

"I'll be damned, a creative nigger, whatever next?"

"Took the words out my mouth, Jimmy. What. Ever. Next."

11

The Donnellys lived in a single story ranch with yellow siding and red shutters. It was down a dead end on an acre plot at the edge of town and where the road ended a tree line began that led to the river.

They had a willow tree that shielded the back of the house from view, beyond which you could see the church steeple and the water tower. An unused swing hung from a low branch. The police station was only a ten-minute walk away, but Arlo always drove.

Hope made sure his car was gone. It had been a few hours since she'd bagged his groceries and he was definitely at the station by now. After this, I'll go to the river, she told herself. The water would look spectacular on a day like today. The waves shining like scattered coins.

It gave her courage.

She took a deep breath and walked around to the back door. The windows were dark. The legs of a plastic yard duck spun in the wind like a cartoon character going nowhere.

Elora had been a few years older than Hope in High School, back when she was vibrant. She had sewed her own floral and polka dot skirts and designed the layout for the school yearbook, but nothing compared to her singing. She had the most beautiful voice Hope had ever heard.

There was talk of her going to college before her father died of bone cancer. It was a sudden and painful death, and after the funeral, Elora and her mother went to stay with family in Minnesota. They didn't know how long they'd be gone.

Mr. Harris, their neighbor, dutifully collected her post every day. A year went by. There were rumors that Elora had fallen into the "wrong crowd," and was spending all her time in Minneapolis nightclubs.

Her mother never recovered and died of a heart attack. Elora returned to Callisto to plan the funeral. Mr. Harris gave her two garbage bags of post to sort through, and so, Arlo Donnelly found her sitting beside a pile of letters on the living room floor. He'd brought over the house deeds for her to sign, and a month later they were engaged.

He was fifteen years her senior and had been married before, to Louise, a good Lutheran until she ran off with the volleyball coach. As soon as his divorce was final, Arlo and Elora were married. People shook their heads with pity, but nobody said an actual word. Arlo was known for his temper, which was good for policing, but not for marriage. He came from a family of mean stock. It was said that his daddy thought nothing of cutting the tongue out of a noisy mule.

Elora made her own wedding dress, and there was no sign of her outlandish ways on their wedding day or any day thereafter. Her dress was ivory lace, long sleeved with a simple V in the front. It showed off her dark hair. She used the same lace to make the curtains in their bedroom window, which just goes to show, everyone said, even a damn warthog like Arlo was worthy of somebody's love.

She got pregnant soon after the wedding. They bought a swing and had a BBQ. She sewed blue and yellow and pink bunting to hang in the yard. She filled little jars with homemade lemonade and gave it to the children to drink with red and white straws. There were steaks, cakes and cigars. Hope remembers how Arlo had kept his hands on Elora's stomach the whole time, proving his tender ownership.

The first miscarriage was public and awful. The church group sent flowers to the hospital, held hands and prayed. The second was talked about in whispers and the third was hardly mentioned. She had become irreversibly tragic. To speak of a dead fetus begets superstition and people avoided it altogether. By then, the curtains were always drawn and Elora would be missing for days, the yellow bruising on her skin fading like a forgotten dream. She never mentioned it. She still held his hand. She said things like, "there's time for us yet," and so people decided to leave well enough alone.

Hope knocked on the screen door. It was open and she peeked in. "Hello?" The kitchen was dark, but for the dim lines of light that laddered the closed shutters. Hope saw Arlo's groceries unpacked on the kitchen table. There was a movement at the table as Elora scurried to cover herself, and in doing so, dropped a towel of ice she'd been holding against her cheek, on the floor. "Shit." She reached forward to grab them, grunted in pain and shook her hair in front of her face, but it didn't cover her eye. It was as round as a black and violet baseball.

"Oh Elora," Hope knelt beside her, picked up the ice cubes and gave them to her. "I'm so sorry Elora."

Elora placed the ice inside the towel and back over her eye. Her lip was split under her nostril and her dressing gown was stained with blood. She stank of heat and sweat. She turned away.

"Don't. Just go away." She sounded a bit like a ventriloquist when she spoke because her lip was so swollen.

"Elora I can't leave you like this. I can't."

"You shouldn't be here." She completely turned around in her chair.

"Nor should you," Hope said.

"You don't understand."

"What's to understand? I can see, can't I? Elora, it's insane! What can I do? Just tell me. How can I help you?"

"By leaving," she whispered.

"I'm not leaving until you let me help you," said Hope.

Elora turned to face her. She looked as though she belonged in a morgue, as though she were a creature, not a woman. Hope had to force herself not to look away.

"This whole situation is driving him crazy. If it could be different, *he* would be different. I know it. I know he wants to change," she readjusted the icepack on her eye and winced. "There is a way. It's a long shot, but I'd do anything. If you want to help, go to Birdie's."

"Mad old Birdie's?" Hope interrupted.

"Do you want to help me or not? Yes. Mad Birdie's. Tell her I need her. Tell her I'm ready now, that I've reached my point, ask her to prepare for me. I'll come tomorrow night. Will you do that for me?"

"Yes, but what will you do in the meantime?"

"What I always do. Just speak to her, please, and swear you'll tell no one. Do you understand? My life depends on it, Hope. No one. Swear it." Her eye looked jellied, fake, as though she could pop it out and bounce it around the room as a Halloween trick.

"I swear."

"Good, thank you. Thank you so much. Now go. Quickly, before he comes back."

Spittle had gathered in the sides of her mouth. It was hard for her to swallow. Her breath made the whole room smell of hot copper. Hope was happy to leave. She had become aware of the shadowed hallway, the shadowed living room and the inability to see beyond a window. She wanted light and moving water. She got up, touched Elora's shoulder, opened the screen door and walked outside. She didn't start running until she reached the end of the road. She didn't want Elora to hear her fleeing across the gravel.

12

Elora stared at the place where Hope had been squatting for a long time, outside she could hear the plastic duck's feet spinning and the irregular squeak of the swing, then she got up and made herself some coffee.

She slowly climbed the stairs to the attic. The roof was pitched and the boxes of her parent's house were tucked inside the places too small to stand inside. She pulled back the curtains of the single window. The swell of her face and its ugliness did not surprise her. It was a face she rarely owned. It changed like a barometer around Arlo.

Actually, it erased. So looking at her reflection was like looking at someone else, it was like feeling from someone else; looking through glass is a way to view things safely. She'd spent years looking at herself through a closed window. Disturbed dust settled in a film across her coffee. She wiped her finger across a box, all of this she thought, the erosion of me, collecting. She balanced her mug on the windowsill, opened a box in the corner and took out a small vial. Against the window it streaked the sunlight blue.

She had used the sleeping powders before, years ago, to ease her father's pain, but also, more recently, on Arlo. "Stuff's like rat poison," she remembered Birdie saying as she mixed it for Elora's father. "It never loses its potency, so keep it safe."

It was not that she wanted Arlo dead, although she'd thought about it often enough, it was simply that she wanted peace in the evening, especially if he was drinking. She'd pour him a scotch, slip in the powder and wait for him to start snoring. Was it so much to ask to walk by the river, to sing, unafraid?

When she was young she had wanted to be a part of something unreservedly magical. Not beautiful, not lavish, nor even perfect, but miraculous the way cave drawings are miraculous, because they prove our capacity to evolve, and lure us into believing our own possibilities. She was tempted by the primal imagination that inspires skill, the ability to dream the initial dream, and then create what has been dreamt. Now, she is only her dreams.

She dropped the vial into her dressing gown pocket and carefully closed the curtains. He would notice something like that; he noticed everything when he didn't want to look at her. She needed to put the groceries away. It was important to keep things normal.

*

Birdie lived near the artist. If Hope followed the river upstream she'd get there before nightfall. Her house was pale green with orange woodwork. Hope knocked on the door and a ruckus of birds flared up. Birdie answered the door with a large parrot on her shoulder as though she were a pirate. She was incredibly small, creased and beautiful. She had gray eyes. She had on thin black trousers, a white linen shirt and a large turquoise necklace.

"Come in, come in," Birdie ushered Hope towards the sofa. "I've just made some lemonade. Hope, is it?" She plumped up the pillows of a rose-colored sofa and sat Hope down by gently pushing on her shoulders. All of her movements were quick and swift.

There was a large brass aviary in the living room, full of parakeets, canaries and a few birds that Hope had never seen before. Inside the aviary were potted plants and small trees. The backdrop was painted emerald green with golden clouds. The room was painted a deep turquoise and red bottles with different feathers stuck down their necks lined the windowsills.

"Sushhhhhh! Sush now!" Birdie yelled. Her voice was large and the birds instantly settled down. "Lord help me I'll get a cat one of these days. Hear that? I'll get a cat," she wagged her finger in the air.

"Get a cat," repeated the parrot.

"This is Franklin. My baby," she stroked the parrot nuzzling her neck.

"Boom. Boom."

"Franklin here loves lightning, don't you, baby?"

"Boom. Boom."

"He knows when a storm is coming. Sit down. Now, we can't talk when we're thirsty, can we? You collect yourself and I'll get the lemonade," she said as she walked into a bright gold kitchen.

Hope nodded. She didn't think she had a choice in the matter. Everywhere she looked she saw large crystals, rocks, piles of books, trinkets and houseplants. Faded oriental rugs covered the floors. On the walls were three textured paintings of large blocks of color. Hope wondered if Birdie had painted them. She returned carrying two glasses and a jug of lemonade on a tray. She saw Hope looking at the paintings.

"It's called Modernism. Do you like them?" Birdie asked about the paintings, and Hope sensed that she'd know if she lied to her.

"I'm not sure."

"I feel the same. I don't *unlike* them if you see what I mean. They were a gift from a client. It's strange. Why three? I asked him. Because of their relationship, he answered. I didn't understand it then, but now, having lived with them for a while, that's the thing I admire. On their own, they aren't worth a damn, but together they're enhanced somehow, same with folks, don't ya think? Some I only like in the company of others," she poured Hope a glass, sat down in a purple velvet armchair. "Now then, I'll begin, so we can escape the boredom of chitchat and rigmarole. Name's Birdie, as you know. The name came before the obsession in case you're fixing to ask. But you know what? We become the thing we're most often called, which will be interesting for you. So. What can I do for you?"

"Nothing for me really. I'm here for Elora, you know Elora Donnelly? She told me to come and give you a message."

13.

Birdie put her glass down. Her eyes were bright pearls inside her pin tucked skin and her face was urgent.

"Elora Donnelly? Really? You just saw her?"

"Yes."

"How was she?"

"Well, she was, she wasn't very good. It was Arlo. He beat her up."

"That bastard. I ought to have him killed. If she'd let me, I'd do it myself," Birdie said. "And the message?"

"She told me to tell you that she was ready, that she'll come tomorrow night."

"Oh! Bless her heart."

"What will you do?"

"Change her mind," Birdie's pearls shone. "It's my special skill. I will change her mind, once and for all."

"How will you change her? I mean, I've heard you were a, you know," she said. "A witch?"

"Yeah, sorry."

"Oh for goodness sake, don't be sorry! I know they call me a witch, I also know they say it like they want to replace the W with a B and that's fine by me. Absolutely fine. Personally, I prefer to think of myself as a symbolic psychologist, but witch bitch will do. I don't believe in magic in a hocus pocus kind of way, that's pure poppycock, but magic in the way that sharing a secret saves it from haunting you. It's no magic really, people have made that word silly. It's just an old knowledge that folks have forgotten. The mind simply works well with symbols and images. Think of Christ on the cross, wedding rings, the lotus flower, the Star of David and so on. I use them to move my clients out of the persona they've created from themselves. Symbols and ceremony, the two oldest tricks in the book. Like I said. It's no miracle really, just the repositioning of power, just plugging the intellect into the emotion," she took a drink of lemonade.

"So you'll just give Elora a symbol?"

"Yes, indeed I will."

"Then what? She just decides to leave Arlo lickety-split?"

"Well, not right away. Nothing but death is quick in life, honey. Even a long death is too quick in the end. It takes time and more time to build a person back from nothing. Think of her like an hourglass. The symbol just flips her over and lets my words, call 'em spells if you like, my words trickle into her like sand, and before you know it, a small mound of self-worth has piled up and begins building a new myth. Poor Elora. She needs a truckload. Hell, she needs a beach. The last time I saw her she was gouged the size of the Grand Canyon. Her body was just a fleck inside her loss. Nothing really, well you know, you've seen it. She was flitting around my garden like a hummingbird. Last winter it was, cold as a witch's tit, pardon the pun, and I was at the window with my binoculars looking for owls and there she was, darting from tree to tree, skinny as a stick, I went and opened the door for her."

"Why had she come?"

"I helped her daddy ease his pain, you see, and got to know her then. God bless her soul. She'd come asking for safety. The way she held her coat to her throat made her hand look like a delicate white brooch. I remember that. She sat by my fire and drank tea and never once removed her hand. It was only when she was leaving, and turned her head to say thank you, that I noticed the red marks she'd been trying to cover."

*

Elora walked beside the stream, baked to a leather map with knife engravings across its bed, until she reached the river and sat down beside the bank. The late afternoon air sat in her mouth like a hot penny. The insects ruled. Their murmur was tidal and scavenging. Elora breathed deeply, she knew about thirst, about droughts of the internal, human kind. Ideas grew in her like seeds under concrete. She relished the dehydrated world around her, for it meant that she was not alone, that the earth seemed merely her body turned inside out and a kinship was formed.

The dirt road that ran parallel to the stream unrolled like a parched tongue and soon Arlo would drive down it, but now she had the river. The current was too strong and low to produce a clear reflection, but it was comforting to see the shadows of her face change. The wind lifted off of the water and felt cool against her swollen eye, like a balm of soothing current.

Behind her the windows of the house looked luminous and she imagined that the house was on fire. In her mind, she burned it to the ground, then stood, listening. I am not stuck, she thought, I refuse to be stuck. She thought about the ceremony Birdie would give her. She could do that.

She could do it for herself. The idea of performing her own personal ceremony made her fate seem less random and suggested control. She could use her voice as a symbol and begin to break the glass.

She stopped and listened. The dusk that was amniotic.

She could hear the reeds slop alongside the mud bank, the locusts and the grasses brushing in the wind. She lowered into these sounds and hummed herself back to nothing.

Her shadow disappeared into the field as though she'd spilled, she soaked and the days heat fell from her in layers, until she was soft. Imagine moss on bone. The last of the sun descended into the water like a retreating red ship.

The night dropped its lump in her throat, it grew and filled her. She could feel her voice, tunneling from far away, yet moving closer, she imagined it shaking the water in glasses as it crunched through rock and soil, it began to burn, to push until it burst and shot up through her legs, her pelvis, stomach, diaphragm, and when she opened her mouth again it slid out, like a burning snake through a snowdrift, it cut and sizzled and entered the prairie.

It hit Jacques in the stomach with the strength of a bullet through a melon.

He watched her singing. He didn't know the song, but it didn't matter. She sang like releasing birds, like mining, like breaking the clutch of sea. He knew that kind of surrender.

The music was her representation. The knife that could cut her away from her other self. This was the voice she had known all her life. It moved around her like salty waves, licked the inside of her shell, glossed her cupped belly to smooth. She reached low and collected its cool shape. She held it close to her ear and heard the world. This was her seashell voice.

That kind of surrender makes you do things just to blur the edges of reason. He dipped below the grass, got down on all fours and started slowly crawling towards her. She heard him, or rather; she heard everything hesitate around him and it stopped her, caught her on its hook. She turned and saw nothing.

It made her run.

14.

"I've got to prepare for her Franklin and it's a sensitive matter, sensitive as a tongue in a jar of burrs," said Birdie.

Trying to help an abused woman was like punching at shadows, thought Birdie. You've got to point your arrow at the beast. Slay the shadow maker. More than that, slay its reason for being. Elora needs ownership of her own downfall, yes indeed, she needs to hold her demise in her hands. It's a reversal of power.

"I hate to say it Franklin, but that woman needs her own penis. I'll tell you what, witchcraft is certainly not for the prudish, but hell, Frankie, nobody is insinuating an operation here for Christ's sake, just a symbol, just a physical thing that she can hold and bury. I know just the man to help," she said as she put on her boots and jacket.

The air was sickly with late blooming jasmine. She planted it when she was young, well, younger, before she recognized the scent as 'old woman smell'. It annoys her now. It strangles everything as well as her olfactory glands. She sticks her middle finger up at the plant and walks on. The Bird. The private alternative meaning to her name.

She found Jacques in the backyard. Dusk had set. His lady sculptures were everywhere. It had only been a few weeks but the house had been painted white and the door had new hinges. The maple tree in his backyard was full of a late summer evening. His garden looked fantastic and he stood in the middle of the rows, harvesting runner beans. She could see small bits of woodchip stuck on his scalp like curly bugs. He looked at her, smiled and stood smearing soil across his jeans.

"Best time to harvest is in the evening," he said and plucked a slug off of one of his plants. "It's also the best time for pest control. How are you *Miss* Dubois?"

"Never better *Mr.* Beaumont. You have a regular harem here Jacques. They are amazing," she turned her palms to heaven and spun around.

"Thanks. Only a few are finished, but yes, I've been busy," he said.

"I'll say," said Birdie as she followed him to the porch. "They have similar features," she stopped to look at one of the carvings.

"Most are of my mother," Jacques said.

Birdie didn't know how to respond, so chose not to, grief was individual and he was an artist, after all. Crickets in the grass filled the silence and the rivers sway. They stood under the roof and stomped the mud from their boots.

"Would you like a cup of mint tea?" Jacques held open the door to the kitchen.

"If you're making one," Birdie stepped inside.

"It's already on its way," he said and removed the singing percolator from the stovetop. He took mint leaves from his pocket, rinsed them under the tap and dropped them into two mugs. "Honey?"

"No thanks," she said as she took the mug and blew into it. "That's nice. Thank you. So. You must be finding Callisto inspirational," she said and nodded towards his sculptures on the lawn.

"Yes," he said. "She just wants to be out."

"Who?"

"My mother," he said.

"Out of what?"

"Her form."

"Right," she took a drink. "Are they all of your mother?"

"Mostly but, a few are of women I don't know. Their faces just come to me and I sculpt them," he said.

"Well, they're wonderful, whoever 'they' might be. So, what's the deal, do you release them through your sculpture?

"Yes," he said and Birdie sensed that he didn't want to explain it further.

"Huh," she thought for a second or two. "That's an interesting idea and related to why I'm here actually. Listen, I need a favor and it's a, how to put this discreetly, it's an unusual one," she cleared her throat and lowered her voice. "I need you to carve me a life-sized penis."

He laughed into his tea. "That's the last thing I expected you to say."

"Don't laugh. I know what you're thinking. Lonely old woman, yada yada, but it's for a client actually."

"No kidding? Exactly what kind of service do you provide now, Birdie?"

"I'm using it as a symbol, like you use sculpture. It's the oldest symbol in the world. The mind responds to an imagined event just the same as it responds to an actual event. Did you know that? The trick is to get the mind working beyond its reason. I have a few secrets of my own, you know."

"I never doubted that for a minute. When do you need it?"

"Today. Can you do that?"

"Sure. Any particular dimension?" He put his hands a foot apart as though he were describing the size of a fish.

"Small, I want it as accurate as possible, no detail, just a thingy and balls."

"Poor man," he said and shook his head.

"Don't say that, even as a joke, don't think or say it for a minute. I don't want any pity carved into this symbol. The man's a beast, an animal, not even a man. Think of that when you are carving it. And when you're finished, bury it under the maple tree out there, doesn't have to be deep, bury it and wash your hands and touch something beautiful. I don't want any part of you involved with this. I'll dig it up. And Jacques, tell no one, not a single soul, I'm serious. A life depends on it."

"I won't, I promise, but tell me one thing: is it for that singing woman? The one with the broken face."

"What do you know about her?" Birdie was taken aback.

"It was just a guess. I heard her singing beside the river and she seemed, well, tragic, I suppose. Impenetrably tragic."

"Let me give you some advice, you stay away from her, I don't really care what you do with yourself, but I am the one and only person in this town that doesn't. Elora is married to the Sheriff," she said.

"What kind of man beats his wife?" Jacques stared past the window to the breastplate hanging on the tree. Elora, he thought, that's her name. It was too late to stay away from her. He had carved her face on the breastplate only yesterday. He couldn't look at Birdie. She was living inside his garden, inside the wood and inside his mind.

"The kind of man that will think nothing of killing you," she put her cup in the sink.

"Point taken. Is there anything else I can do for you Madam Dubois?" Jacques bowed extravagantly.

"Come to think of it, yes. Could you also whittle me a small woman? About pinky finger size?"

"I'll make sure she's singing," he said and winked.

15.

At midnight, Birdie found the small woman and the tip of the penis poking through the soil like mushrooms. Birdie pulled them out with ease and put them in her pocket. The lightning bugs set off the locusts' alarm. There were chimes on the breeze and the smell of dirt and split wood. His carvings waited in the soft apprehension of midnight and shadow, where the sky ensues evergreen and the moon lays broken across the river.

Whatever is happening has already begun, she thought, so be it. She walked towards the river. But there was no harm in asking for guidance.

"Help me," she said to no one, to everyone, to everything.

*

The following evening, Elora poured the sleeping powders in the scotch and waited. Arlo came in through the back door and she could tell by the way he struggled with his boots that he'd already been drinking. He needed courage to see me, she thought, and she was right, for when he saw her sitting at the kitchen table he said, "Oh baby, just look at you."

He knelt down beside her. "I'm so sorry. I could just kill myself. This whole thing is crazy. This situation, you know, it damn near makes me crazy," he put his hand on her knee.

"That mine?" he nodded at the scotch.

"Yeah," she said and handed it to him.

"I don't know what I've done," he said and took a swig, "to deserve a woman like you. I love you Elora, you know that don't ya?"

She nodded and stood. She'd heard it all before.

"You hungry?"

"Starving. I'm so sorry, baby," he said and necked the rest of the glass. "What's for dinner?"

"Pot roast," she said and took it out of the oven.

"Smells good," he sat down and she dished him up a big helping.

They ate in silence and when he'd finished, he wiped his mouth with a napkin and said, "I think I'll just go lie down on the sofa for a little bit. It's been a long day."

She nodded and started tidying up the dinner plates.

He was snoring within a few minutes. She went into the living room, stood over him and watched him until she was certain he wasn't going to wake up, then she grabbed her coat and softly stepped out into the night.

The land was spread like a palm before her, a hand waiting to snap shut and for once, she thought, she might be able to escape its grip. It was a matter of time, she told herself as she walked along the river towards Birdie's. Time waited inside her like air in a bottle, invisible to the naked eye and heard only when breathed into, when turned into music.

*

There was a time when she'd been young, which was a laughable thought, because she was only twenty three now, but when circumstance fast-forwards the heart, the age of the body becomes irrelevant. When she had yet to be weather-beaten, had not yet found her place inside of peace or denial and believed that the order of things could change with little sacrifice. The want of youth is as merciless as the regret of age, both injuries, one the sharp stab of impatience and the other, a slow leak. When she was young, she spoke like diving.

"Daddy, I can sing," she said.

"You get that from your mother. She can sing."

"I'd like to be a singer, Daddy."

"She can bring down the angels above with her voice, that woman, she can make you cry."

"I'd like to study music at college next year."

"I remember a time in Boston. We were dirt poor. Your mother said she'd had enough of living on love and potatoes. Said, 'Tonight we'll eat steaks' then got up, walked out the door and stormed down the stairs. Just like that. With that crazy look in her eyes she'd get when she fixed her mind on something. I just let her go. I thought, what now? But the next thing I heard was her sweet voice rising up from the busy street below, rising up to the open window and resting right there on the windowsill like a goddam spring robin. I kid you not. It wasn't even two seconds and I heard the first coin drop. That night we had enough money for two steaks and some greens. Lord we feasted like we'd never done before. Decided right then and there to move out to the land of the plenty."

"But Daddy…"

"Just stop right there Elora, there's no sense romanticizing about the impossible. You just pull your head out of those clouds and be happy with the life the good Lord gave you. It ain't a bad one. You hear me? It ain't bad."

16

At home, Birdie lit the wick of a glass hurricane lamp. They would need it for the burial. She has always preferred them to modern flashlights because of their glow and primal flickering. It was like reaching back through time towards a memory she felt at ease with but couldn't quite grasp.

She put Franklin in her bedroom and warned him not to peck the curtains. She put a blanket over her aviary and listened to the birds adjust their wings for sleep.

It was not going to be easy, earlier in the week she had spoken to Stan, an old friend, about hiding Elora if necessary. Of course he agreed, and although she didn't expect a massive change from Elora right now, it was the first step, and Birdie wanted to be ready. She patted the wooden penis in her cardigan pocket, if this doesn't scare her off, she thought, I might just have a chance.

Through the open windows she could smell and hear the pageantry of the night, and then Elora's hesitant footsteps on the path that lead to the house. Birdie went to the door and opened it. Elora's face was wet and crazed. She didn't say hello, she just walked straight in, sat on the sofa, and with great care, folded her hands in her lap. Her eye was as mean as a canker sore and her nose was starting to scab. Birdie moved the hurricane lamp to the coffee table beside her and she glistened with moisture.

"Hello Elora," Birdie said and Elora turned her face away, the lamp outlined her sharp profile. "You sure you want to be here?"

Elora shrugged. "I do. It's just. Difficult."

"I imagine it is. You're very brave to have come in the first place."

"It feels dishonest. But, I have to do something."

She said nothing and put her hand on Elora's shoulder, Elora flinched, then relaxed into her palm. "Let me get you a drink? A hot tea or a glass of wine?"

"Wine please."

"You have every reason to be nervous. I don't blame you one iota."

"No, but I blame myself, otherwise it would never have come to this."

"What do you blame yourself for?" Birdie handed her the wine, she took it and Birdie sat down across from her.

"I don't know. Being empty, I guess, emptiness."

"We all empty out sometimes, Elora. We'd become stagnant otherwise, and stagnant water can turn to poison. What you fill yourself with is important."

"But I've tried, I've tried to fill myself with goodness, happiness," her face began to crumple. "You don't know how I've tried."

"No, I don't, but listen, let's not make this so huge, it becomes scary," Birdie could tell she was losing her, could feel her retreating. "You're here now. It's good to chat, as for anything else, we'll go easy," so you'll come again, she thought. "I've just planned a little exercise that will plant a seed of power in you, and if you let it, it will grow to replace your emptiness," Birdie poured herself a glass of wine and sat down next to Elora.

"How do you mean, "grow"? Like a baby?"

"Yes. Exactly like a baby. That's a wonderful way to think about it. Your own beautiful healing baby."

"Then maybe I'll be able to carry a child?"

"No. I'm not promising that. I make no guarantees I can't keep. You'll have a seed of power. You can try to use it any way you like, as long as you don't use it against yourself. That's the condition. Do you agree?"

"Yes. But I'm not sure I can leave him."

"I'm not asking you to leave him. That's not my decision. I'm simply asking you not to use your new strength against yourself."

"Okay."

"Good. Now. I have to say this, Elora; I wouldn't be human if I didn't and although I'll only say it once, the offer will always be there. Do you understand that? Forever. Should you decide that you needed to leave, I have a safe house for you with a friend of mine in Chicago."

"He wants to change. He hates himself for, you know, for it," said Elora.

"By 'it' you mean 'you' correct? He hates himself for hurting you?"

"Yes, but," she took a deep breath.

"But?"

"But if I could just have a baby things would be different. I know it."

"Yes. Things would certainly be different. There would potentially be two of you to hurt."

"I am not here to leave him, Birdie."

"I understand, but you need to tell me why you're here. Why did you send Hope?"

"I don't know exactly. Like you said, to heal. So that maybe I can, I don't know. I need a change, we, we need a change. I want to make a change happen." She took a drink of wine.

Birdie looked at her for a long time and made her decision.

"Okay. Okay, let's make it happen then. Here," she took the carved penis out of her cardigan pocket and handed it to Elora.

Elora let out a breath of surprise. "Is this?"

"It's what it looks like. It's a penis, tackle, dick, Johnny boy, knob and a whole lot else, but get over all of that nonsense. Just rub that out of your head," she wiped her hand across Elora's eyes. "What you are holding is also one of humanity's oldest symbols of masculinity, virility and fertility. And that, my dear, is how we are going to use it. As a symbol, pure and simple."

"Oh," Elora took another big gulp of wine. "What exactly do you want me to do with it?"

"Relax honey, you don't need to brace yourself. I simply want you to hold it and breathe deeply through your nose. I'm going to count backwards from ten, and when I reach one, you will be in a state of relaxation, like a trance or a dream." As she spoke the words her voice softened and lowered. She had done this many times before and recited with confidence: "You do not have to do anything against your will, but the words I use, and the ritual you perform, will remain inside your mind, where you can access them instantly for strength," she began counting.

Elora closed her eyes. Her face was almost wet with moisture as though she'd been swimming through the lamplight.

"Hold it and think of it as the symbol it is. Now make it weak and empty, like a limp, hollow worm in your hands. Have you done that? Good. Now think of your past as a map and begin to unroll it until it extends all the way to your childhood. Look at it. It's like a long inscribed road with fields and timber and valleys and the Mississippi. See the town square, the red barns, the church, and the park with the swings, the school. Everything is there. Can you see it? Wonderful. Now, light up the people and events that have caused you pain. Make their lights bright and visible. Take your time. And when you're ready, raise them above the map, so that they're floating. Let each one rise, tell them goodbye and let them fly towards and enter your symbol. Fill that symbol with all of your pain, your anger, your loss, your fear. Is it completely full? Is it shining with light? Good. Now, turn it off. Turn the light off. Snuff out every little glimmer, until it's dark and dead, like a stiff corpse in your hands. Now we are going to walk outside and bury it because it's dead. Are you ready?"

Birdie took her satchel from a hook and opened the door to a vivid night. Elora followed her. The lamp lit the cobwebs on the grass. They walked through damp to the riverside. Elora cradled the symbol like an infant. Birdie knelt and took a trowel from her satchel.

"Look at the river," Birdie said. "The river is constantly reshaping the banks that define it. People can do that too. We can reshape the way we hold ourselves to enhance the way we flow. Stop blocking yourself, Elora. Are you ready to let it go?"

"Yes."

"Then take the trowel, dig a hole and bury it."

Elora dug a deep hole.

She placed the penis inside and covered it completely. She wiped her hands on her thighs and sat staring at the river. Her eyes were lit.

"The pain does not own you anymore. It does not control you anymore. It has no power over you. It's weak and limp and dead. You killed it. You will replace your pain with your own strength. You will become strong. You are the one that shines now. You are the one full of light. Now, when I finish counting forward, you will reach full consciousness where you'll feel stronger and more able to manage your life."

Birdied counted her back to consciousness and after a few moments of silence, she took the geode from her satchel and handed it to Elora.

"Open it," she said.

Elora opened it and found the tiny carved woman inside a bed of crystals.

"That's you," Birdie said and took her hand. "From now on, remember, no matter what happens, that's you."

"Thank you," Elora said and began to cry.

*

Days passed and Birdie's words were a current inside her. During the day she did not sing. Daylight was like a licked finger and thumb that extinguished her and inside of its hours she became unidentifiable to herself, as if she'd been sucked dry, a raisin, a shrunken head, but with a mouth that formed words, with arms and legs that followed instructions.

She stood in front of the mirror and touched the skin healing on her face. Sweat made it sting, but it remained unbroken. Her face had gone from broken to unbroken. Once again she looked like the sheriff's wife and people could treat her with as much indifference as a tin of pineapple or Spam. She perpetuated their indifference by wearing a public face that was both agreeable and undemanding; a pretty mask that worked in a way similar to how birdsong disguises the cruelty of wilderness.

People felt safe around her, so she was able to keep herself hidden, and those in hiding know how to listen and the more she listened, the more she understood that the skin was often a rug that character was swept under, like dirt. The skin, the body, was immaterial. When she dared to believe in anything, she believed in music, so it was no surprise that Jacques arrived in song.

17.

It was hot in the car, even with the windows down; it was like breathing though a steamy washcloth. Arlo made her wear stockings to church.

"Ladies wear stockings," he said.

They had laid towels across the vinyl seats so the back of their legs wouldn't burn. Her towel was wet with sweat. Arlo draped a towel over the steering wheel and started the car. Elora stuck her head out of the window and the breeze was like the harassing breath of some animal. Her face had all but healed. As soon as they reached Highway One the dust stopped.

"Thank goodness for that," Arlo said. "It'll be good you getting out and seeing folks. They have been asking how you were," he put his hand on her knee and patted it.

Highway One was a paved road that shot straight through the heart of Callisto, splitting the two halves of the town like an apple on either side of its asphalt. A finger snap of white wooden houses, enclosed by river and prairie, snugly tucked inside the clapping blue waves and flowering virile grasses that kept Callisto hidden, mirage-like amidst a feverish green. Unparalleled freedoms existed inside such seclusion, but dwelled as all freedoms dwell, inside their own shape of entrapment, so Highway One was a necessary emblem for the mind as well as a convenience for the body. It was a way out just in case one wanted to use it.

Arlo preferred the back roads; the intertwined dirt paths that he'd helped to carve and level. The dusty and insensible tentacles that lead to ponds, to cabins, to shacks, to overgrown groves, fields, homesteads, to the river, to nowhere and dead ends. Taking Highway One was a Sunday exception, because Arlo washed the car on Sundays and wanted to keep it as clean as possible for church. "Cleanliness is next to Godliness," he would say.

Every Sunday there was a moment of breathlessness as soon as the wheels touched the highway's spine. A moment where the uneven jerk and pop kick of gravel became a purr, smooth and easy. It made leaving seem easy. A simple course of action, like licking an ice cube back to water, a steady and smooth movement inside which time would alter the entire consistency, the entire nature of the thing, of her. It seemed so easy and she imagined herself jumping from the car, running all the way to the interstate and hitching a ride to Chicago. Her mind caught in the whirl of motion and dreaming.

Then the sight of the white cloud-popping steeple and Arlo slowing the car to avoid the fling of gravel's rock as he pulled into the parking lot and the white wooden church, square and stout with three stained glass windows that ran along either side. The shape of the windows mimicked the steeple, arrows pointing up; pointing in the direction death would take you if you'd enter. The front door was a simple unpainted oak and above it a round stained glass window, blue with a white dove holding an olive branch in its beak. They walked beneath it. They were always early.

She stood there trying to smile. She was too hot inside her knee length skirt, her long sleeved shirt and stockings. She straightened her spine uncomfortably. It was hot as hell and everyone moved in slow motion, as if they had each been bitten by a poisonous spider, and the heat was turning their insides to liquid. She imagined them all melting, dolloping through the cracks in the floorboards like mercury.

The sun streamed through the windows, a torch behind a slice of colored Swiss cheese, she felt dizzy. Rainbow prisms shifted across wooden pews and the white walls and she felt as though she were inside a kaleidoscope. It spun. She spun. The edges blurred and rounded, spinning, spinning then black. She fainted. She collapsed like a person without bones, no person at all, a doll, that fell and fell through a black gelatinous dream.

It was the dream of a play already in motion.

She was a single drop of water that began to vigorously multiply, three of her, then five hundred, sixty thousand of her split, divided and filled like a cloud, until it became a forceful gray throttle and released. She dropped, crisp through the sky, a glass arrow headed for the earth's throat. A million of her followed, mirrored droplets, inside each one the watery reflection of her face, ten million faces, twenty million faces, plummeted and smacked and folded through the musky sucking mouths of soil. Rain, and with it, erosion. Fragments of her pushed as one, all of her faces carved, forged, split rock and push towards the churning deep and blue.

Then. A slap, not hard but intending. Her eyes opened. Above her their damp faces relaxed and softened from worry.

"It's okay, folks," Arlo said. "It's just the heat. She's just fainted from the heat." He held a damp dishtowel against her forehead.
She felt sick.

"I feel sick," she said and they backed away not wanting vomit on their Sunday shoes.

She was woozy.

"I need some air," she said and they backed further away allowing her girth to rise.
Arlo helped her. "Steady," he said, "steeeeady now."
As though she were a horse he was leading into a stable.
"Steady, girl, steady."
She pushed his hand away. "Just give me a moment."

She walked towards the door. The dove in the window glared at her; its yellow eye seared a hole in her forehead, while behind her the Reverend clapped his hands.

"Show's over people, let's return to our pews quickly, quickly now."

The organ began to play and she could hear her Arlo's laugh. He was happy. It had gone well, she had performed and he had gotten away with it. He was already talking to someone about fishing. She opened the door and stepped out into a colorless womb of dust. A veneer of dust covered over everything like camouflage. A tree was not a tree, but dust in the shape of a tree. The bank was a brick square of dust. She wanted to hide as well, so walked across Highway One and into a deep ditch, where she laid down and waited for the dust to cover her.

Then Jacques.

Jacques stood above her, looking down with curiosity and not judgment. Neither one of them were startled.

"There you are," he said and with one hand he helped her up to standing. In his other hand he carried a bunch of purple clover.

"It's for salad later," he said.

Hair, black. Eyes, black. And skin. His body was large and strong against the sun, his body sharpened the sun. Jacques.

"Your face has healed," he said, bent down and touched her temple with his thumb. "Are you alright?"

What could she say? He was open and frank. "Sometimes," she said. "Not really," she turned away. "No."

"Come on," he took her hand, "I've something to show you."

They walked through the field together. Gray clouds umbrella above them and raindrops began to bounce off the dry earth like clear rubber pebbles, an instant shattering of bullets. Thunder cracked and opened a waterfall, at once, they were washed, baptized. Their beginning began with the drought's end, began with a flood. It was like this: she wanted to sing, then she met Jacques and there was song, wretched song.

18.

The fresh rain mixed with sweat in the folds of her skin. It caught in the hair on her lip and slid into her mouth like hot tears. She could feel dripping everywhere and mud, slick and gritty between her toes, filled her shoes. She stopped to tie her hair into a knot on top of her head. She stared at his hands, wrinkling with rain; she could not meet his eyes, but sensed him looking, thinking. They sloshed down the weed-worn track and all the way to the house. The storm was loud and crackling. He motioned for her to follow him around the back. She could see the river was dimpled like wet gray silk. They stood under a canopy of maple leaves. The raindrops fell heavy and irregular against their heads, against the wind chimes. In the watery blur she could see flashes of red and yellow vegetable and berries. She could smell onions.

"Wait here," he told her. His feet smacked against puddles until he disappeared. The rain let up a little and the sky lightened.

She noticed she wasn't alone. Wooden sculptures of women were everywhere, watching, enclosing, a small army of goddesses in every size and shape. Some were tucked away, others were standing or lying on the ground, some were hidden in bushes, amongst the branches and the rhubarb, one was on top of the house, in every corner, carved women. Some were useful, were benches, chairs, one beside the back door had outstretched arms and hooks for fingers. Some were pregnant, were one-eyed or half-fish, half-bird, half-wolf or were half-buried. None looked finished. They were all crude and hovering with the sense of the unmade. She shut her eyes. The noise they made combined like a murmur, no voice singled out, no one thing heard or identified, no song.

"Ready," he said. He was holding a carving the size of a breastplate.

It was a large single wing with her face chiseled in the center. In it, her eyes were closed and her mouth was open. In it, she was singing. She felt speechless.

"Do you like it?" He smiled a white crescent.

"Yes, of course I do, but, how did you know about the singing and," she hesitated, then brought her hand up to her face.

"I heard you. The other night by the river. No, wait, don't get embarrassed. I understand it, where it comes from, that feeling of being out of control of your body. I know it."

"I knew someone was there. I was afraid."

"I know. I was too."

"Of what?"

"Can I?"

He didn't wait for her to answer, he untied the knot and her wet hair fell and smacked against her shoulder. It was a sound that stopped everything. Like a gunshot, a child's cry, a turning doorknob, water. He brought his mouth to hers. She felt them watching, trees trapped inside bodies designed by his hands alone, and turned away. They desired him, she could feel it, they craved him and she felt as though they were closing in, from the beginning, felt doomed by his sculptures. She knew they wanted to be human.

"I'm sorry," she pulled away. "I can't."

19.

She ran back through the field and rain poured from the sky. The exhausted earth lifted and opened in a hazel gratitude. What had been dry was filling, feeding again. Lightning and thunder in the sky and inside her chest. He was the artist Arlo had told her about. Jacques.

Dust settled and the world seemed green with possibility. Outside the church, children were dancing in puddles and a hot vapor rose from the reawakened ground. Elora stood beside the car in the parking lot and let the rain pelt down upon her. She wished it was acid. She wished it could melt her skin and make her someone new, someone that could walk away from her life and into another, without fear.

The church bell rang. In minutes the parishioners would run from the door to their cars. How could she reenter her life? She touched her lips. He had already washed away. We are still thrown, she thought, even the dead, even me, live inside an impulse we had imagined was impossible. The galaxy still explodes above us, redefining, reconfiguring the course of things. I want to be new, she lifted her face to the rain, make me new, she prayed to the sky.

"Have you lost your mind?" Mean eyes unlocked the car and opened the door. "Get in the goddamn car and use the towel. People are staring. Jesus, woman," he said.

Inside the car it was silent and warm fluid drained from her ears as if they'd burst. Arlo drove. She could tell he was searching for words. His hands wrung the steering wheel.

"I don't know what's gotten into you. Half the time I come home to find you staring at the river, or a tree or space like you're in a coma or something. Now this, standing in the rain, catching your death, in front of everybody. Don't you have no pride? I know things aren't always good between us, but that's just folks, that's just marriage, rough and smooth, but goddammit, Elora, you have me at my wit's end acting like a crazy woman," he paused.

Elora watched raindrops slide down the window. He parked the car in their drive, turned the ignition off, and looked at her.

"I know I shouldn't drink so much, but I gotta lot to deal with, keeping the law and, well, coping with you. You ain't an easy wife, Elora. This ain't an easy life. A man has things he wants, a good and sane wife, a family, sons. Half the time you don't even give me a proper dinner. I'm not complaining, I know you got things on your mind, but I want you to know that behind every action there is a reason. I love you though. You know that," he turned her head to face him. "You're still the prettiest girl around, so I'll keep ya, crazy or not," he said and laughed.

*

The rain did not stop, it didn't even slow down, so that what was moist and alert began to droop, saturated and oppressed against the bloated ground. It collected in the wires of the screen windows like cells of a dragonfly wing when magnified. Like loneliness, Elora thought of things that fly and die within one season, of Jacques, sweeping in, and then, suddenly visible. To see her face in a wing. To feel captured, and let go, at once. Soon the soil will swallow no more and the fields will swell until they spill over. Like me, she thought. Tonight, as soon as Arlo left for his card game, she'd walk to the river.

*

Jacques stood at his bedroom window with the lights out. He could just see Elora beside the water's edge. Thinking about her was like driving through a storm. It took concentration. Few things arrested him in such a way. He made the decision to see what would happen if he drove through to the other side, walked down the stairs and waited for her with the front door open. He could see that she was holding the small woman he'd carved for Birdie.

"That's the second carving I've made of you," he called out and she stopped on the path. "Did it work?"

"I don't know," she said and walked towards him. "I'm sorry I left the other day. I just..."

"Don't be. It's okay. Everything will be okay."

She sighed heavily.

"'That world inside your sigh, knows no home'," he quoted.

"Who said that?"

"I can't remember, somebody. Why don't you come over tomorrow and I'll introduce you to my sculptures. Who knows? Maybe you'll make some new friends."

"Wooden friends," she laughed a sad laugh.

"The best kind. They know how to keep your secrets."

20

Arlo left for work and Elora ran all the way to Jacques's house, past the sculptures and up the porch steps with muddy calves. She knocked on the door.

"You came," he said as he opened the door. "Come on in, I'm making breakfast."

She was breathless and her hair stuck to her face in lashes. The large windows in the living room cast rain-speckled shadows on the floor. She stepped from square to square and followed him into the kitchen. Her socks left wet marks that absorbed unnoticed. Jacques was making eggs and coffee. He put a large dollop of honey into his coffee and stirred it.

"I eat everything with honey now. The flowers are different here and the honey tastes like sun," he took a sip and flipped his egg. "Aren't you going to talk?"

"This place," she touched the walls softly. "It's like I've been here before. I can't explain it," she circled inside the sundrenched emptiness. "How did you know to buy it? In town they say that you bought it unseen."

What difference does it make to the condition of the mind if a place is real or imagined? Remembering is a form of imagining that fastens the mind to a place, and real or unreal, it's the place that matters. The place is where the identification is made. When Elora walked into Jacques's house she identified with it immediately. It was in part the image of her personal landscape. The image of her escape, of her as free.

"That is true. But I knew it was empty, big and isolated." Like you, he thought, "I knew it had a view of the river and I understand that scale of lonely."

The words lonely and understand in the same sentence were like a cleave to her inhibition.

"They also say you are an artist." A statement, not a question, she had seen his sculptures of course, but wanted to legitimize him.

"That is also true, as you know."

When the emotions came they arrived like a herd.

The heart's fabric is the filament of dreams. He pulled at the very seams of her, pinpricked and unraveled her until she stepped out of her skin and into midair. She could see where she wanted to land. She could see who she could become.

"Would you like to see them?"

He lead Elora to the back door.

He tucked his sculptures like artifacts into the foil of his person, where they stayed with him persistently, like faith or guilt. So that, for him, the act of creating was a form of tracking, tracking his secrets, claimed and unclaimed, following footprints and branches as broken as dreams, until he met a pair of eyes. Until he saw himself. Meeting her was standing unafraid in the middle of his wood, where all of his animals lived, some peacemaking, some deadly, but all of them ravenous. The idea of loving her was like entering the incalculable fold of time and eating through layer after layer of sediment, becoming, inhuman with the power to save.

Outside, his sculptures bloated with water. He had positioned one by the window, and Elora stood beside the glass and looked at her. The grain had begun to split like a hoof up the center of her body, she had no arms, just a neck and head like a clothespin.

"It's like she's peeking in." Elora drew a circle in her breath mark on the window.

"I know," he said. "I like that, but I can move her if it bothers you."

"No. It's fine. It's just, different, that's all."

"Different good or different bad?" He put a plate of fried eggs on the table.

"I probably shouldn't be here," she said.

"But you are. So maybe you should just have a seat and enjoy yourself," he handed her a fork and pulled the chair out for her to sit down.

For a while, they ate together in silence, then she asked, "Jacques, what do you know about me?"

"I know you're less, far less, than you should be," he said.

"And you know about my husband, Arlo?"

"Yes," he said. "But that doesn't bother me."

"Why?"

"Do you want the truth?" She nodded, yes.

"Because I imagine that the part of you that married Arlo is the part of yourself that you don't love, but want to heal," he reached across the table, took her hand. "That's not the part of you that I'm interested in. I want to know the woman that I heard singing, the woman that Arlo doesn't recognize and, perhaps, even fears," he said. She burst into tears.

He slid off the chair and kneeled beside her and took both of her hands. "That's why I carved you, twice. My specialty is to resurrect life and, believe me, there are as many ways to live as there are to die."

*

He was a sculptor. He brought things to life. He could carve a woman's body from a dead tree. He could carve a rosebud from a dead tree, a cathedral, a rabbit, a soldier, a wand, but he chose her.

"How long will you stay?" She lay against his chest, his heart in her ear.

"I don't know. As long as it takes, I guess."

"As long as it takes for what?"

"To finish them, release them and feel the need to leave."

"Your sculptures? What will you do with them?"

"Leave them. They belong here."

"But they're yours," she said.

"They're nobodies, casings. They're practice."

She opened her mouth to speak, but he put his finger over her lips and slowly unbuttoned her shirt. She was stunned. It was as though she were someone else, had entered another's body. She let him undress her until she sat naked in the late morning light.

He lifted her arm above her head and traced the slope beginning at her wrist and curving all the way to her hipbone. He lifted her hair and placed his finger on the bone behind her ear, moved it across her hairline, then down to the end of her spine and around to the front of her waist to her navel. He circled her navel three times, then moved his finger up, and traced each rib. From there to her breasts, he circled the girth of each breast before he traced her collarbone, her neck and jaw line, then shoulder, he drew a circle on her shoulder before he moved his finger down the outside of her arm, past her elbow to her hands, he spread and moved between each finger. Then he did the same between each of her toes and circled her anklebone, traced up to her knee, circled, circled then lifted her leg and pushed her gently back. His finger drew circles on the thin skin behind her knee before it traced down to the soft underside of her thigh and down, down.

"I sometimes imagine myself as water," he whispered as his finger entered and traced the inside of her.

"I look at the log I'm about to carve and imagine myself as water and the log thriving once more from my nourishment," he circled her.

"This is what I need. To give life again by taking the decayed away, weakness away, to be the hands that offer reincarnation. That resurrect another form, another you," his finger moved in deep circles.

She could not speak.

"Yes," he laid his body on top of hers, "what I want," he kissed her open mouth, breathed each word down her throat and one by one they entered her.

"What I want is (inhale) to (inhale) wake (inhale) you."

*

It was foolish to fall in love with a man who could envision himself as water. For such a thing could never be held completely, instead longed to hollow caverns, forge with rivers and respond to the tender dry slurping of roots. The thing we most need to contain, to live and churn under the moon, enters, shapes and slips away. Sometimes she could see him clearly. She could see his watery body shoot like a transparent bullet, through trees, through her, sculpting rings, small historical sentences of antiquity, he was the ringmaster. That is what he was. The Ringmaster.

21

Months had passed, and although Jacques carved his mother, she never resurfaced. He tried carving her in every possible way. Perhaps she wanted to die. Perhaps she'd given him Elora instead. Elora had become the focus of his carving, his living resurrection. She was visiting him regularly now and he could think of nothing he wanted to sculpt more than her form.

Sometimes his gift felt like a dream and he had to test that it was real. He rigged a few traps behind his shed. On the second night he caught a fox. It was dead by the time he found it, which was fortunate, as he'd always harbored a soft spot for the creatures. It was cruel to catch it, but he needed to be sure of his gift. He released its floppy neck, took it inside and laid it out near the fire. The evenings were cold now and his hands would cramp in the air. He wanted this carving to be accurate. He placed a small dish of milk next to its head so it could drink when it awoke. It took one attempt. He placed the sculpture on the hearth, opened the front door and watched the fox skitter out into the mud-colored evening.

A large thump hit the window behind him and he walked into the living room where the collision of the kestrel was powdered across the glass in a delicate sketch. As though the bird had hit the window at such a speed that its ghost had been knocked from its body and captured on the glass. He opened the window and looked out. The bird with the broken neck lay at the base of the house. He picked it up and held it. His mother was near, her presence perfumed around him, and it struck him that without his thoughts, this bird would carry no meaning, his mother would remain dead. Only ideas give significance to forms and light. He stared at the bird until its name vanished, then he laid the bird out on the table and began to chisel a piece of chestnut. All the while, he felt certain his mother was blowing into the kestrel as though it were a feathered bellows. Inside each of us lurks the thing we did not choose, he thought, but what is chosen for us. One day a catalyst for it appears. One day, death. One day, love. Art. And then, you begin.

*

Jacques. Every second. Jacques. She spends afternoons in the garden. His skin still inside her fingernails, she longs for soil, to dig and plant. It is too late for flowers, so she plants bulbs and the idea of things growing beneath the surface, the idea of flakes of him feeding the spring, these thoughts have no data, these thoughts develop as instruments develop the first time they're played. Which is to say that they ripen into the music they were born to create.

She enters the house and washes her muddy hands in the sink. Arlo, comes up behind her and sticks his finger inside a black bubble. He smells of beer and stomach acid. He pushes his cold hand up her shirt and presses his pelvis into her thigh. She can feel his holster against her leg.

"I thought you were going to go fishing," she said.

"I like watching you in the garden," he whispers in her ear and pulls her head backwards so that he can kiss her on the mouth. Compared to Jacques everything about him, his skin, his tongue, his movements, is sloppy and rough.

She forces herself to turn and face him, but he stops her, reaching around her waist and lifts her skirt. She lets him. She is not his. What he takes is mere fluid, tears, blood. Salt. His violence is not the violence of evolution, but of the underdeveloped and crude. Outside of herself, of his invasion, she is developing and the world all around her is embryonic. It is the place where birds defy the ground. Where she is sky.

For Elora it was a time when things were made, not destroyed. After Arlo left, she sat on the porch and watched the leaves red as blood fall, singularly, like pinpricked drops filling the garden one by one. There was life developing inside her. She unwrapped the ideas she'd bandaged, her memories, so that light could get through and grow. She could feel the growing, growing.

*

"Do you think she saw me?" Elora asked.

Birdie had been to visit.

"Yes, but she'll keep it secret," he said and put his arm around her. He smelled of soil.

"What did she want anyway?"

"Nothing much. I think she was out bird watching and just stopped by to say hello. Are you hungry? Because I'm starving."

"I could eat. Are you sure she won't say anything?" She put her arms underneath his chest and hugged him with her cheek against his back.

She knew she ought to visit Birdie and explain her relationship with Jacques, but admitting it to another person made the danger of what she was doing seem real. She wasn't ready to deal with that yet.

"One hundred percent sure. Do you have time for a sandwich? I made some bread."

"I think so, a quick one."

"I wish you didn't have to go."

"I know, so do I."

"Just a minute," he ran outside quickly and came back with a fistful of basil. "Cheese, tomato and basil perfection." He put the basil to his nose and breathed deeply.

"Here eat this. It's been lovingly prepared." Elora sat down at the table and bit into the sandwich. Jacques took a pitcher from the refrigerator and poured two glasses of iced tea. He raised his glass.

"To us," he said.

"To us," she took a drink. "Tell me something."

"Something."

"About yourself, your past," she took a bite of her sandwich.

"Like what?"

"Like, I don't know, anything, like why do you have polished spoons, yet only two shirts?"

"You want to know about my cutlery?"

"Nobody uses the word 'cutlery' here," she said.

"I'm not from here," he said.

"I know. I love that. But it doesn't answer my question. I feel like there are so many things I don't know about you," she wasn't ready to tell him that she was pregnant, not yet, not until she was sure, but she felt the need to unearth his past.

"The story of my cutlery is a marvelous tale actually. It's deserving of an ode. Ode to the Beaumont Cutlery," he said and raised his sandwich like a sword.

"See? This is what I mean. You avoid my questions about your past."

"I'm not sure what you're truly asking, and besides, you might not like what you hear."

"Of course I will. I just want a bit of history. A bit of, I don't know, understanding."

"Okay. See this spoon? I once found it poking out of the garden like a sliver carrot."

"I'm serious."

"So am I."

"Why do I love you?"

"Because I am mysterious and leave you full of wonder?
Come here," he pulled her arm, she got up and sat on his lap. "Be patient with me."

"I have to go," she said. "Arlo will be back soon," she stood to leave and he grabbed her arm.

"I'm sorry," he explained. "The spoon was my Mother's. She buried the cutlery in the garden when she was losing her mind. It's hard for me to talk about my parents."

They were, distant. Preoccupied."

"So the sculptures," she said. "So that explains the things you can give life to."

"You have no idea," he said.

"Maybe. But I'd like to."

"Stay the night," he said.

"What about Arlo?"

"He's not invited."

"I'm serious, Jacques."

"So am I. Drug him, hell, kill him. Do what you need to do."

22

After she left, he sat at the kitchen table and picked up the spoon. It was true. He had actually found it poking out of his garden like a silver carrot. His mother had emptied the contents of the utensils drawer onto the floor. He remembers that everything had crashed but the cutlery. It was missing.

Jacques and his father had been sitting in the living room. Jacques was reading and his father was looking at his maps. She had taken a handful of flour down from the cupboard and started sifting it onto the floor like hen seed.

"What are you doing?" Jacques said.

"Catching footprints. Someone's stolen our silver," she said and looked up as though she'd actually seen someone.

She leapt towards the corner and her flour-covered fingers ripped apart the air. Mathis stood up and took a deep breath. He grabbed her by the shoulders and wrapped his arms around her as she lurched towards the invisible thief. Jacques had tried not to look at her, but she was glowing irresistibly. She always shined during a fit, as if she'd been scrubbed clean.

"I need your help," Mathis said. "Grab her legs and let's lift her to bed."

Jacques bent down to take her legs and she kicked him square in the eye.

"Jesus Christ!"

"That's right! Shout! It feels good to shout!"

Jacques and his father began screaming and Nora joined them. The three of them screamed until their heads ached, then they flopped down on the kitchen floor like panting dogs. He remembers how the flour had stuck to their nose hairs.

"He stole my silverware from France," Nora whispered to Mathis. "Kill him."

"Ok Nora, I will," Mathis said.

He stroked her short hair. It had grown quite a bit and her scars were nearly covered. She fell asleep with her head in his lap.

"What will we do?"

"Find it," said his father.

"That's not what I mean."

"I know. Help me get her up."

They carried her to bed. His father's grip was emblazoned on her flour-dusted arms. She was as thin as a wishbone under the sheets. Jacques remembers her peaceful face and how they had stood watching her.

"I don't think it will be long," Mathis put his hand on Jacques's back. "Come on.

Let's find that cutlery," he said.

They searched everywhere for the spoons. In the larder, in pots and pans, linens, under loose floorboards, in the woodshed, the commode, everywhere when Jacques finally remembered that he'd seen her, days earlier, scoop away a bald patch of snow from the vegetable patch. She had poured a kettle full of boiled water over the uncovered ground.

They boiled the kettle, grabbed a shovel and stepped out into the cold night. He'd seen her standing underneath the charms she'd made to keep the birds away. The charms hung as still as wooden icicles. Sure enough, as the hot water melted the soil they could see little shiny handles like silver carrots poking through the ground. They collected the cutlery without saying a word and walked inside. Jacques's hands were so cold that they burned when the warm air hit them, he stood thawing for a moment by the fire, while the sensation of pins and needles spread across his body. His father wiped the cutlery clean of mud, polished each one slowly, thoughtfully.

"When I showed your mother these she just stared at them. They were like shiny jewels to her. It physically pained her that I ate with them. Once I came home to find the house decorated with cutlery. I have to admit it was beautiful the way they sparkled, I laughed and laughed, sure my father was turning over in his grave at the thought of cutlery on the mantelpiece or hanging from the doorframe. You see, your mother and I are similar creatures; we share the same curious eyesight. We both can find magic and luster in what others find ordinary. I love her for that, for many reasons, but most of all for that. I'm telling you this because it's how I want you to think of her, treat her. Even when I'm gone. Do you understand?"

The following morning his father blew into his hot cup of coffee and closed his eyes to its steam. The logs cracked and burned steadily and the room was silent, but for their little sips. They did not look at one another when they heard her feet slap across the floor, the water pour into the bowl, her hands gather it and splash it across her face.

He had tried to think of something else, tried to think of a happy time and remembered, as a child her strapping him across her back like a snug, little cub and the three of them snowshoeing through winter mornings. He remembered his parents holding hands and the snow falling, like powdered sugar, dusting over them all. When she entered the room her hairline and eyelashes were still damp.

"Morning, well, this is certainly a day for porridge," she said cheerfully and filled a pot with water. She opened a drawer, "Ah, my silver, I've been wondering where it got to."

23.

He thought of Elora and his mother and love. He made a pouch with his shirt by lifting the end hem and scooped up the cutlery from the drawer. He walked around decorating the house, forks on the mantel, spoons on the windowsills beside the geodes and knives on the bookcase. He put them wherever the sun shone, so that the light would have something to strike as it moved around the house. He thought of light like this, as a solid thing, as a block that he could press a shape inside.

He had learned to manipulate light from his father. To his father, light was something to hold, direct and capture, but to him it was a life force to break and redirect. He had taken life, had broken light and placed his shadow, as the image of himself, in front of her stream, however frail, however weak, like a blockade, he had made the final decision and it filled him. He could bring the shadows back.

He looked around the room. Everything had a reflective quality, the geodes, the cutlery, even the piano bounced and outside, the river, brown and muscular, reflective, yet moving as though something were thrashing underneath and he understood its violence. It was as thoughtless and shaping as the light. It was not the violence of war, but the relentlessness that poisons the marrow enough to fight. This he was trying to mold. This he was trying to cut into. One snap of peaceful transcendence, one snap of an independent world.

The source of radiance is often hidden. Was Elora this source for him? They certainly kept one another hidden. Their relationship revolved around the fear of truth, rather than its embrace. There was something that he couldn't reach. A meaning that seemed to constrict every time he is close to touching it, the worm of his childhood, small as a blood vessel, that used to vanish inside the coral whenever his hand drew near. It kept him from telling her about his ability to resurrect.

She approached singing in the same way he approached sculpture. At first, he believed that this would allow her to understand his gift, but the truth was that her singing produced nothing physical. He could create life from death and that fact would always separate them, but he wanted to tell her about his mother.

Did that mean that he loved her?

It wasn't love in the way that he had anticipated love. Yes, the lust was there, yes, the heat and excitement, but perhaps he just wanted somebody, anybody beside him. Somebody he didn't have to explain things to, who hadn't the courage to ask and delve. No, courage is not the right word. She had courage. He couldn't deny her that. She was risking everything for him and yet, there was something else. It was as if she had a vested interest in keeping him only the man of her perception. He had to be the right type of savior, the bad prince, but a prince nonetheless. She would never leave Arlo for a murderer. Is that what he was? No. With one hand he had taken away, but with the other, he had recreated. He had done his mother a service. Would Elora, or anyone for that matter, see his actions as benevolent?

It was better not to ask, not to risk breaking the illusion that served them both. He had told her the truth about the spoon, she could have pushed open the answer, but had decided not to, he felt, so that he remained safe inside her need to keep him perfect. There is nothing luminous about a man with faults that he can control.

In truth, he was a dry rock, and her devotion, her body, was like the water that made him glisten. He was ideal for her. The only flaws she saw in him were the ones he could not change. And as for him, he needed someone to hide inside, so love like a blanket to a prisoner. They were each other's perfect escape. At first he welcomed her desire, of course he did, he was starving and she longed to be devoured. He wanted someone to touch without cutting and we are drawn to people with ideas as big as our own. It was hand-in-glove chemistry, but now? Now she was trying to make him real, and reality suffocated him. Inside reality he found no air. He had come to believe that air was something he needed to create.

He was ashamed to admit it, but the sense of relief he felt after his mother had died was enormous. Her life had become a jaw that snapped around him, and then it was over, and he was floating, momentarily in his own air lifting off the ground like a dragonfly unclenched and let loose. Or maybe something bigger, like a balloon or a cloud, anyway, he was beginning to feel free. It was shameful. It was so unlike him. Actually, that's a lie. It was just like him. He despised neediness, weakness. It made him feel as though he was shrinking.

He doesn't want to lie himself into another life that's wrong.

He's always felt as though he'd been stuck inside the wrong body, the wrong mind, with his own flickering nature too buried to excavate. Thinking of her feels like choking on the dirt of himself. It's far better just to carve new figures, new bodies, chiseled out of his own rock self. Sometimes he wonders if he might just find one that resembles the actual him. He doesn't mean this in a sentimental bullshit way. A piece of wood with his face trapped inside it eager to revitalize into something else. He's talking about the flow and stacking of atoms here. He's talking about sculpture as exploitation of space, where he would assume the space that was meant for him. The shape that fits. When he disposed of his mother's body he felt atoms buzzing around the emptiness like flies ready to reconfigure.

How could he tell Elora about his gift? Would she understand? If he loved her then surely it would be something he would want to share with her, right? He was afraid that it would always divide them and she would grow to resent what she couldn't possibly relate to.

His time now, in simple terms, is the occupancy of collage, what to keep, what to take away, what to hold, what to push, what he allows to harden. That's one of the reasons he finds sculpture so seductive, for no matter how flawless the image, the wood will always succumb to forces beyond his control. She will never be what he expects. Like love. Love is also the beginning of erosion, in terms of the perfect self, but think of the beautiful shapes erosion has created. It's why he likes to keep himself fluid, lava like, it lets him carve the space around himself in the hopes that one day he will crystallize into a shape he has created, then erode.

*

If his sculptures could speak they would say:

We took to the wind like wooden birds, we wanted to lie down and anchor beside him. He had found us tangled and overgrown, limbs shrieking in the night. We were already falling when he caught us, a hook in the belly of a rolling log; it was just in time, just in time. We thanked God. When he began carving his vision, we let him, grateful for touch. During the stages of becoming we grew confident and whispered our desires like spells, please, please make me a woman, a crane, an angel, a mermaid, a horse, ibis, ibis. And he listened. Chiseled us out like blown eggs. In the beginning we were as full as we'd ever been. He seemed a life giver. The gift of rebirth. Then the air began to circle us like it'd move around a cave, chilling and hollow.

24.

Jacques went to CC's first thing in the morning. From the moment he stepped foot in Callisto, he felt noticed and watched, as though a crow were following him. She was right. If they stayed together, they couldn't stay here. Perhaps they could run away to Chicago or some other wilderness? Maybe she could give him whatever it was that he needed? He was stuck between picturing his life with and without her.

Birdie constantly came over with extras, meat mostly, and with his garden, it had been enough to keep him from town. He hadn't prepared for this type of exposure, but couldn't turn around for home now, as he felt that would raise suspicion. For what? He wondered.

The door chimed when Jacques opened it and right away he saw CC chewing on a toothpick with his arms folded over his chest.

"Well now, looky here, it's our own bonafide Frenchman come out of hiding."

"Hiding?"

"That's what we thought. We thought you was hiding yourself or something from us."

"No. Just working, that's all."

"That's what I hear. I hear you're an artist. Some kinda wood maverick, but hell, even a working man's gotta eat."

"I have a garden."

"Must be one helluva garden. I hear that old bag Birdie's been helping you out as well. She's madder than a hornet near lemonade."

"She's been really kind actually."

"She's a witch you know. Got to watch out for witches."

"I don't know anything about that."

"Doubt you'd say if you did."

"Maybe we should start over. My name's Jacques Beaumont," he went to stick out his hand, but CC waved him away.

"I know your name, son."

There was the usual stuff on the shelves and Jacques put tins, toilet paper, meat, milk and eggs into his basket. He was desperate to get out of there. A young girl with Lucy written on her nametag stood behind the counter and rang up his purchases. She went to bag his groceries when CC cleared his throat to get her attention. She looked up at him, he shook his head no and she handed the paper bag to Jacques with eyes full of apology. He bagged his groceries and walked towards the door.

"Nice to meet you," he said to CC.

"Yep," CC kept his arms folded across his chest as Jacques balanced the bag on his hip and opened the door.

Pig, Jacques thought as he stepped out onto the sidewalk. The bag wasn't heavy, but it was cumbersome and he wished he hadn't bought the biggest pack of toilet paper. The day was warming up and he had a long walk home.

He walked down Main Street. A few of the shop fronts had been recently painted. Rosa's Café had a green and white awing. On the window was a painted wreath of red roses and Arlo's face looked through it straight at Jacques. He was sitting in his usual place buttering his toast, watching the small world. He saw Birdie's Buick Skylark roll to a stop and hoot the horn at Jacques.

"Never let a good-looking man walk when you can give him a ride," she winked.

He laughed and approached her window. "Don't you ever stop?"

"Lord no," she said. "I have to remain deserving of my reputation. Moral disgust is my disguise. Now, get in."

"A business woman through and through," he said as he opened the door and arranged his bag of groceries. "Thanks. I'm not sure how I would have managed this," he nodded towards the toilet paper.

"Shit always gets in the way," she said and winked. "What in the world are you doing in town anyway?" She looked accusingly at his groceries.

"I could ask the same about you," he said.

"Yep, you could, and I've been at the bank, but it's different because I'm not sleeping with anybody's wife."

"Yet."

"I'm serious here, Jacques."

"Right. You caught me."

He rested his forehead on the glass. Silos scattered across the green fields like pieces from a wreck. He pictured a machine world above the clouds aborting the broken parts of itself, heavy things falling from the sky.

"They can't do anything to me," he said, finally.

"You're a damn fool. Their granddaddies could have had you arrested just for walking Main Street and you don't think that's bred in? They are just waiting for an angle and if you weren't rich and connected, they'd have run you out by now. Listen. You're lucky. You want to sculpt, so sculpt, and stay outta sight and mind if you want my two cents," she stopped for a breath.

"Do I have a choice?"

"Not unless you like walking. If you want another two cents, stay the hell away from Elora, I mean it, I feel it, let her down gently, but let her down. It will only end badly. Arlo will kill you both."

"What if I told you I loved her?"

"Love's a fluid thing, Jacques, especially when lives are at stake. But if that's the case, you need to disappear. And quick," she said.

"Elora wants to us to run away to Chicago."

"Does she now? Crafty little vixen. Well, if you're gonna run, you better run further than Chicago, think Mexico, think someplace where they'll never find you, because if you take his wife, and they find you, you'll live together for eternity."

He said nothing. The sound of the road pinched him like a tight belt. She pulled up to his house and he could barely breathe.

"Don't tell me if you take off. Just go. The least amount of lying I have to do the more convincing I am."

25

Birdie sat on her porch and watched the day draw itself into evening. There was a weeping in the smoky sky, a spasm of red and orange, her heart, her stomach, told her that something was about to go wrong. Across the field, she could see the shadowy figures of Jacques's wooden idols. A sculpture stood beside the river, then moved, and Birdie watched as Elora crept up to the back of the house and knocked on the window. Jacques opened the door and the girl blazed inside his grip. Birdie stood, walked inside and began preparing an invocation.

*

Jacques kissed her neck.

"I can't believe you are here," he said. "What happened?"

"Arlo got called to testify in a court case in St Louis. He'll be gone for two nights. Can you believe it? God," she said and looked up at the stars. "It's such a beautiful evening."

"Yes, it's the perfect evening for a concert," Jacques said and kissed her again. "Come on. Everything will listen."

So they set about preparing.

Clues of the rain's battering remained in frogs, fallen crops, fat creeks and mosquitoes, and the sulfurous smell of hot decay rose from the prairie's humid bottom. The grasses were straight spines of lime green that twitched against one another. Elora stepped down from the porch and into the field towards a patch of thistles. She could just see their tall purple heads spiked against the night sky like bee stings. She loved the pride of a thistle, how it could be both hard and soft at the same time, like the face of a porcupine or the gloss of polished metal.

"Elora," he called, running to catch her, "you'll need these."

Panting, he placed a pair of garden gloves into her hands, then bent down, broke the flowered head off a bit of white clover, popped it into her mouth, and walked away. She chewed its sweet gum all the way to the thistles, then squat between the grasses and bent the base of a thick stem until it snapped, releasing its sticky milk. She brought its gentle speared flower up to her face, and felt a tremendous sense of relevance that she wanted to remain, rightness, the ant crawling up her arm, the heat releasing from the prairie's marsh like a velvety lotion upon her bare legs, the moon in the sky, everything in its rightful, willful place, even his reluctance to give all that she wanted, and her resignation to take less than she needed, seemed the right imbalance. The child inside her was a small presence. She would have to wait to tell him, for she couldn't bare it if she lost the baby and broke both their hearts.

She gathered the thistles together and walked back to the house. She placed them in a jug and put the jug on the piano. One by one, Jacques was hauling his carvings into the back garden. He placed them in rows.

"Looks good," he said, appearing once more from behind the house. Under his arm was the wooden figure of a woman with fish scales for skin, her closed eyes and mouth were shaped like crescents.

"I'll wheel the piano out in a minute," he said, placing the figure in the yard next to a plump naked woman with a featureless face and a wreath around her neck. "After we eat."

Earlier in the day he had pulled from his garden carrots and onions, and put them in a large terracotta pot with a chicken and some garlic. It had roasted all afternoon and filled the house with a delicious smell. He had picked a big handful of spinach, runner beans, some tomatoes and coriander, cut them up and stuck them in a bowl. His rhubarb was ripe and delicious, he chopped it up and baked a cake for dessert.

"Can you take the cake out of the oven?" he called from inside his workshed and emerged with a large rectangular block of wood. Elora saw the beginning chisel marks of legs and what looked like a cat's tail.

"No need for her to miss out on tonight's festivities just because she's in the womb," he smiled and caressed her, then stood her beside the figure of one whose arms were left as branches. His wooden audience was in place.

Jacques moved a small end table out to the porch. He placed a piece of cut chicken on each plate and a helping of spinach salad. He poured two glasses of wine. Elora stuck a fork in the cake cooling on the countertop. It was clean when she pulled it out.

"Come out here and sit down," he said from the door.

When she stepped outside she stood still for a moment, paralyzed by the view ahead of her. He had placed each woman side by side facing the porch, so that there were three long lines in the yard looking like twenty wooden soldiers. An audience of warfare goddesses and behind them a wave of black and a fractured moon.

*

The sculptor removes. He takes one thing and makes it another by eliminating what he deems as unnecessary. He manipulates space, and it is true, there were things he chipped from her that she did not need, that she was better off without, such as the presumption that human beings are any more divine than other forms of life. Yes, we are the thinking creatures, the planning creatures, but what of the instincts we have lost and suffused?

This is what he gave her.

The removal of calculation and the introduction to instinct, which gives way to the soul, just as the chiseled piece of wood reveals the curvature of a neck, and an air that swirls like a lick inside it. Spending time with him was like blowing away sand and uncovering a body hidden beneath. The soul preserves, waits for you to find it, and waits for you to engage.

*

"Tonight we'll give them a show they won't forget," he said taking a bite of chicken. "This is delicious. If I do say so myself."

"What songs will we sing?"

"Any that come."

"Inventive singing. My favorite. I feel sorry for our audience though," she said.

"They'll love it," he said. "They've served their purpose anyway. I'm done with them now," he said and put down his fork.

"What does that mean?"

"It means I've done all I can for them and you're the only figure I want to carve," he got up and wheeled the piano out onto the porch.

She laughed and sat down on the chair beside him, single chords struck the dark like random splashes. A prairie night is a riot to the unaccustomed ear; you have to adjust your breath to hear through its clamor, slow your breath to hear music. It gives nothing away and forces you to pay attention.

"Are you ready?" he said.

"Yes, but I don't know what to sing."

"Just stand up and open your mouth," he said, "I'll play the sounds to follow you."

The porch felt like a stage. Above her the clear night loomed in waiting and the stars, a million animal eyes shining against a black as far-reaching and meditative as a deep sleep, and the carved women ahead of her, softened by their shadows, pearl like, waiting for her to begin, so she opened her mouth and nothing. Nothing. She opened it again, left it open, until a sound swirled up the back of her throat and fizzled its way out like a dying firecracker, a struggle.

Jacques struck a piano cord, a middle C, she followed it, hummmmmm, breathed it in and out until it became an incantation. Hummmmmm – then higher – open aaaaaaaaaaaaaaaa – louder, louder still – a low and sonorous uuoooooooooo and the atmosphere began to give back. The atmosphere oscillated between her voice and the air's own wide bellow, they played, catch and throw, catch and throw.

It was not as before, no bone fork in her throat, no thunderous musical revelation, but rather an eager partnership between the air and voice, like the steady tension that vibrates between would-be lovers, and each thing bounced on this taunt thread compelling her to sing its human name, so that she stepped out and sang every part unto her, and every part came alive and the night, a stirred dust, collected in her droplets of wet eyes, tongue, lungs. The tanginess of time, the taste of mold and rust, particles rose up and settled, coating both colossal and microscopic, each arched blade of wheat and each burst of pollen, the curve of every petal, and the angled pockets where leaf grows outwards from limb and the sky, a black drum pounding.

It activated everything. Everything.

Shifted. Electrified. Hummed.

She called their names, their own essence – mosquito, mothwing, cricketcry, ragweed, cornhusk, riverslurp, thistle.

She called herself, she called him, playing behind her his collection of notes that flowed and scattered like wildebeests, heading towards his carvings, his women, their audience, she sang them alive for him like a gift. Their anxious figures, tenderized by their shadows, chewable, no longer wood, but meat and flesh. One by one. She called them out of themselves – fishwoman, hoofedwoman, snakewoman, cat. They rose with bones of air, straight into his heart of lush, lush unearthing, of discovery, they walked, she walked, calm as a believer approaching a terrific storm, that power.

*

They ate every drop of stew, ate every crumb of cake, drank every drop of wine and then one other. Thank you. Thank you. Thank you. She whispered. Then later –

"I love you," she said.

"I know."

"It's true, you know it's true."

"What we know changes."

"But I can feel it; you must feel it, don't you?"

"What we feel changes."

"Stop talking like that! You're the one who believes in instinct, right? There must be no greater instinct than the instinct to love."

"Survival forms instinct."

"Then I need you to survive."

"No."

"Yes."

"Let's run away together."

"Where do you want to go?"

"Anywhere."

"Someplace where we can be together. What about Chicago?"

"It's not that simple."

"You make it difficult. We could easily melt away in Chicago, live forever."

"Look, nobody says forever and means it, okay?"

"I do. I'd stay forever."

"You don't know that, forever always grows into something else. I'm telling you, it changes."

"Then we'll grow together, move together, change together. I'll follow you."

"Yes. A part of you will."

"Which part?"

"The part you let me take."

"Take it all."

"No. That's not how I meant it."

"It's what I mean. Take all of me. I love you."

*

In the middle of the night she woke. His arms around her, his mouth, his weight, the weight of a loan, then sleep, his shadowed face turned from her. His cheekbone lightened with blue light, on it were two pockmarks, like craters in the moon. He was like the moon, that close to the body. That far away.

26.

It is remarkable how the heart can become the sum of a life and the body just a way to feed it. Touching him was like placing her hand through a cool running stream to grab a piece of gold she'd seen sparkling there, elemental, elemental to a fault, not a love a human can sustain, not a love that can want, but must remain as is. This is the deception, and yes, when she met him, her truth split and revealed only the brightest half of itself, like iron before it cools into a gray shape, and this was the truth they lived in, formless and molten. She could not ask anything of him, no detail that would place him inside of a mold, no clues, nothing to hold, there was only now, he'd say. But what he meant was, that with no hint to a past there can be no indication of a future, for one needs the other to see. She thought this was artistic, adventurous even, and at first, could not recognize its cowardice, for a life will always find someone to take responsibility for its existence. That is what lives do.

For him to remain molten, she had to become the shape of his steel but first to melt, the embrace, the melting, the time spent in her liquid state, when any form seemed possible, any carving, any casting, any shape and so, she was content to just flow around him like water in a bottle, to run off his body of ideas like a fast-moving drip.

Even her fear of Arlo was diminishing. She now lived in a place beyond his control where her body could create a new life. Little soul, she whispered to it daily, stay with me. She wanted to tell Jacques, but couldn't, as though voicing the words would make her lose the baby. Also, there was still a distance about him, as though he inhabited a space he had not shown her.

It was the way he spoke of the present that made it pliable and unlocked from the past or the future. His disguise was freedom, like a religion; so holy he guarded it to the point of devastation. But too often devastation is mistaken for revelation. She felt guilty for wanting anything solid, so guilty she spoke only of things no human could catch. Stars. Songs. Plants. Time. Impossible things. Impossible when you realize that nothing indefinitely needs you.

A child grows with or without you, love lives with or without you, and hate, nothing needs you, nothing but your own will to create a miniscule space for throwing life into, a hole in the ground, a net in a tree, hands leaking water, but sometimes, sometimes you get the sensation that there is more than survival, and a collection of disappearing firsts. Yes. Sometimes you feel a pattern flash inside of you with no memory behind it, no future ahead of it, just a perfect moment wanting nothing more than to live itself out, and you think, this is mine, mine alone. Singing inside the night's intimacy was such a moment for her.

Only these flashes, these instants can be kept; no person, but there was once one she would have died for; no idea, but there were many that she dreamt; no song, but there was once one that'd been sung; no thistle, but she had once held one in her hand.

Somewhere she knew this, somewhere she knew that ownership was not a concept nature recognized, and had she thought about it, she might have been able to retrieve this inborn knowledge. Perhaps then, she could have swelled with the peace that comes from allowing each moment to be just what it is: a moment among a series of moments among lifetimes, were it not for the terrible power of desire. Of human want. Terrible the way the most cherished things are terrible; terrible the way all that is worth living for is also terrible – because as soon as it enters us it becomes human and to be human is, inevitably, to end.

It was sunrise when Elora got home. He had parked around the back. The trial was postponed because a member of the jury had had a heart attack. He was waiting in the dark house, beside the shutters and their ladders of light. When she opened the door, he grabbed her by the neck and the geode she'd been holding crashed against the floor. The small woman fell out of it.

"What the hell is this?" he kicked the carving with his foot.

She couldn't answer. She couldn't breathe. He recognized the carving as Jacques.

"A nigger whore? Is that what you are? A nigger whore?"

He tightened his hands around her neck. She kicked and scraped against the wall until she stopped. He let her body collapse onto the floor like a marionette. He wiped his hands on his uniform.

He stepped over it and picked up the carving from the floor. The rims of his eyes were red with hate. He put the carving in his shirt pocket and poured himself a whiskey. He sat down on a chair and looked at her. Shit, he thought and grabbed a kitchen towel and dropped it over her face. He couldn't have her looking at him, not when he needed to think.

He walked to the garage, flicked off the security light and scanned the room. He'd take her to the river. He took the tarpaulin off his fishing boat. She'd fit under it nicely and the town knows how much he loves fishing, so nobody would think it strange.

He took his wallet from his back pocket, removed an old slip of paper from behind his driving license, read the telephone number and dialed.

"It's me," he said and cleared his throat. "I'm sorry to wake you, but I need your assistance. Can you get a group together by tomorrow night?"

There was a silence while he listened to the person speaking on the other line.

"That's right. Well, you know I can't be involved. You'll find him at the old Zimmerman place, Beaumont's his name. And Harold?"

He poured himself some more whiskey.

"I'm asking you to get old-fashioned."

*

Jacques needed stones for the eyes, perfect polished river stones.

Elora had left before sunrise. His craving for her that night had been ravenous. She was like a trunk he wanted to cut open, thrust open, and with his tongue like a chisel, he severed her and severed her, until she was small enough to swallow with one bite. All day, her scent coated his hands and arms as he carved. If he could have chewed the wood, he would have, it was his first real sculpture and it was of her. But there was something missing. Something retrieved and of the earth, he knew it, and so, the river stones.

He went to the river and he dug through the mud, and he felt the soil and thought of her moisture. The trees cracked in the wind, black branches on black water, he looked and saw her pretty mouth gasping beside him.

A fish, he thought, a mermaid, crawling up the riverbank towards him. Her name did not arrive and he stepped out of himself and into someone he recognized as dangerous.

He held the stones in his hands, one on each palm – eyes – he had always thought of his hands as eyes. He could see with them. Like a gift, they had led him to her. Her eyes were flat black. He winked his hands at her. He noticed red marks were already around her throat. She lifted her head towards him and he felt it was a sign. He carefully placed his hands and fingers along the marks, like letters, inside the script provided. It was perfect. Now she would be able to understand him, to know his gift.

"I'll bring you back," he whispered into her wet ear. "And I'll love you. This way, we can both escape," he said and squeezed until he felt it leave.

It was delicate. There was nothing thunderous. It was like easing a cork from a jug, she just went pop, and it was over, done, drinkable. The air was drinkable and he tipped his head back and guzzled it all, drank until he bloated with unearthly desire. I can bring her back, he thought, and with his fingers brushed her hair clean of sticks and pine needles, before he folded her into the river, and the river took her, soft as a tissue. He put the stones in his pocket and felt free. Free.

28.

Birdie threw a cardigan over her dressing gown and slipped her feet into her work boots. All day, her mind had felt as twisted and cramped as an octopus inside a small cave. The moonlight was pulling her out of herself with a beckoning. She grabbed her binoculars from the hook as she walked out the door. The sounds outside were like lamentations and she knew that her restlessness had meaning behind it.

She walked alongside the river towards Jacques's. The lights were out and his goddesses were all standing together like a mythological army. She held her breath as she walked past them. She was heading towards a copse of pines just beyond Jacques's house. The trees led all the way into town, black evergreen wings like a gathering of dark angels penetrated the sky.

She had seen a nighthawk there last year, nighthawks were two boomerangs tied together with a body and nearly soundless, but for their insect diving. The air whirled off of them as though they were small steel aircraft. It's been a good year for mosquitoes and there was a pool of water near the copse. She stopped and listened for the plummet of wings. The grass was wet and buggy. She should have worn tall socks. She scanned the trees through her binoculars. Nothing. Nothing in the air. Everything was still, too still.

She scanned the river.

It looked as though a log had caught itself on a slab of rock that jutted from the bank. She walked closer. The river was somnolent and trapped sound against her reservoir. Birdie watched the water cover and uncover, cover and uncover the hand as though it were a water lily, splayed and out of grasp. The white root of arm descended towards a head of hair that danced, almost separately, from the body that tapped against the rock, until it unlocked and was carried away in a swirl.

At first, Birdie denied what she had seen. It seemed too graceful to be tragic. The way the body had moved appeared deliberate and alive. Elora. Birdie ran to the side of the rock. There was nothing. No torn cloth, no blood, just a spin of motion in the water hitting the bank. She closed her eyes and squeezed them until she saw red shapes. No, she thought, no, but there it was, resting on the needled floor amongst the pinecones. The tiny carved woman. She picked it up and wrapped her hand around its shape as thin as a finger. She let out one cry and ran.

*

She pounded on Jacques's door. He opened his bedroom window and peered down.

"Are you alone?" He couldn't see her face, but her voice sounded cracked and raspy.

"Yes," he said and she burst into tears. He ran down the stairs.

"Hey, hey, hey," he said as he led her by the shoulders through the front door. The river woman was lying down on the sofa; the dark stones were set into her hollow eye sockets. She was the size of a torso. He picked her up and gently placed her on the floor. Birdie could hear him talking to her in soothing tones. He stroked her forehead. Her face looked like Elora.

"Her eyes are drying," he said and motioned for Birdie to sit down. "Birdie breathe, whatever it is, trust me, it will be fine, just breathe," and he took a deep breath to show her how. She followed suit, the two of them sat in silence taking and releasing breaths until she took his hand and kissed his palm.

"Listen to me because there isn't much time. Arlo has killed Elora. I saw her body in the river. You will be next or get the blame. I found this," she showed him the tiny woman. It was clutch indented into her palm. He took it and rolled it around in his hand as though it were an object of infinite mystery.

"This must be her gift to me," he said and looked over at the carving with love.

"What?! No! You are not hearing me. I know it's a sudden and terrible thing, but you need to listen! Elora is dead!"

"No, Birdie," he said soothingly and took her hand. "She's not."

"She is!" Birdie snatched her hand back and slapped him across the face. "Wake up! She's dead and you will be next! Arlo will kill you. I'm telling you this because I want you to live."

"You're right. I need to live," he looked again at his carving. "It's important that I live."

"Yes," she said and started, once more, to cry. "I am so sorry. I never should have asked you to get involved, to carve for me. I will die with this sorrow, this guilt, I will die with it. But you don't need to. You can go. You can erase. The sun will be up soon. Pack a bag and I'll drive you to St Louis. Take a train to anywhere and never come back."

That's what I'll do, he thought, I'll ride trains, I'll carve, I'll be free, but when he opened his mouth he said, "Elora."

"You will find someone else. You're young, believe me."

"I carved this for her," he knelt beside the carving on the floor. "I can't believe it, but it's true. She led me to her, to my carving," he had the eyes of a fanatic, rollicking, black dots inside of whitecaps. "It's the first one that's ever been real. I can't leave her."

"Elora or the sculpture?"

"Both."

Birdie looked at the figure lying on the ground. The river's water had soaked a stain around her eyes. He had put the stones in wet, she thought, as though the woman were crying.

"If you stay here you will die," she said, sat beside him and took his hands in hers. "You will never sculpt again. Bring her with you."

His face was more alive than anything she had ever seen. It was its own planet.

"You're right. I'll bring her to me," he said and stroked the grain of her cheek. "I have that power now."

"Okay," said Birdie. "Okay, but we need to leave. I'll bring the car around. You pack."

She drove him to St Louis where he caught the Burlington Northern Railway up to Chicago and then on to Canada. They drove through the final colors of the night with the windows down to drown out the silence. The city seemed to calcify against the horizon. Jacques had rolled up his window and motioned for her to do the same, she did, and the molecules between them turned to gel. He pushed, slow and difficult, he pushed his hand through the space and stopped, fingers spread, in front of her face.

"See this hand," his eyes, his voice both calm and wild. "It can do anything. I can bring her back, but she will need to recover."

"Who?"

Jacques gave her a hard stare before he spoke. "You know who. When you see her, tell her to find me," he handed her a piece of paper with his Pine Creek address on it. "Make sure she comes for me Birdie. The best way for her to recover is to create something phenomenal. I'll do my best to fill her, but I might not be able to do it all on my own."

She dropped him off at the train station. He looked exuberant. She remembers thinking that. He's exuberant and lifted. Everywhere she looked the city was steaming, gray. He passed through the concrete swift as a bird's shadow and disappeared. On the drive home his shape remained in the seat beside her like the presence of a dream. She realized she was trying not to think, that thinking made her shake. What did he mean? Worse yet, who was he?

29.

Jimmy brought her post. She held it in her hand. It felt remarkable that ordinary things remained. She stirred herself into character. Harlotry as camouflage.

"Where you been?" he asked her, the engine of her car was still hot.

"Visiting Stan."

"Who is Stan?"

"My sexy boyfriend. Why, you missed me?" They knew she had a sweetheart whom she never, as a rule, spoke about. She did it to throw him off and it worked. He raised his eyebrows in feigned surprise.

"What? I might be old, but I ain't dead, Jimmy. Nature has endowed him, if you know what I mean, *and* he has a motorcycle," she swung her hips from side to side.

All suspicions of her implication were completely squelched inside of his embarrassment. Inside parts of her were breaking away and whirling, a pile of leaves left for the wind. Be done, she thought, I need sleep.

"Well you missed one hell of a show."

"Yeah? You doing the whiskey dance at the tap again?" Sleep.

"This is serious Birdie, serious. Seems your neighbor was a full-blooded dark horse. He killed Elora Donnelly and then himself. Guess they were having an affair."

"No," she stared past him at the feather white clouds, the words spoken out loud crashed against the bits of her hanging in the blue. "That can't be true."

"It can and it is. Arlo found his body a mere few hours ago. Sent him back north. Some say he wasn't completely dead when Arlo found him, but you didn't hear that from me."

"And Elora?"

"Still looking for her, but her clothes washed up a few miles downstream. He refuses a funeral for her though, can't blame him, gonna have her cremated and tossed in the river. She's got no folks to protest. Fish food, that's what he calls her now, but hell, you can't blame him."

She closed her eyes and took a deep breath. "God help us," she said to the sky.

"Seems to me he already did," said Jimmy.

*

Jacques took the train. He placed her gently in the seat beside him, his gift from the river, he'd take her home to Canada. He was worried he couldn't completely turn her.

After her initial awakening, she had remained caught inside death, a butterfly beneath glass, and he feared that she might never return. He spent the train journey etching her an inverted leaf dress and long sinews of river hair. The veins in the leaf simulated the veins of the body, and the stem was a chain of tiny pearls that wrapped around her throat like a necklace. It was only when he carved a baby in her arms that she sprang to life as a butterfly, waiting, still as death, will unexpectedly beat against the window.

The window was his eye, he opened it, and that's when the frost beneath his eyelids began to spread. And although her rebirth was fleeting, momentary, he knew her resurrection had occurred and any future sculptures he would create were ways of developing her and coloring her in. He knows she's out there and he's drawing her, carving her towards him.

The stars were silver filings in the night. Chips from something hard and cold, metal or bone. The motion bump, the flash along the track, a nerve along a spine and the houses dissolved, her soft face with its windows dissolved into the water, fading, shading the wind, her body drawn with charcoal on his and gone.

He felt her scattered.

She came to him as an after-image, as though he'd been staring at something illuminated, then closed his eyes and waited for the retinal image to appear.

He felt her in the silver filings.

The other bodies and his, a magnet, they flung against. Coating him, sharp foil digging in a shard of shine until he felt like someone new, someone heavenly, all at once, alive.

He wrapped his arms around the carving and propelled life through his skin, gentle and chilling, he brought Elora forward.

30.

Pine Creek, Canada 1953

Mathis had followed her trail, claw raked of twisted bush and littered with fresh scat. The air was thick with the smell of digested fish and hung like a canopy of moisture above him. His skin chewed with insect bites. Moss hung in green cloaks from the trees. He followed the trail her enormous stomach had rolled through the pine needles towards a keyhole of light.

She was staggering. She bashed against branches. He looked up and saw the mountain gnarl the sky. Splintered teeth on soft gray flesh. He was gaining elevation and the sodden air began to crystallize and break from heavy to fresh. Snow was on its way. He turned around and looked behind him. The way back was a dense darkness. He looked forward and the keyhole glowed. He was clumsy and weak as he stumbled through it.

Her cave was as small and black as a nostril.

He entered the smell of rotting death, and there she was, a breathless boulder. Dreams die when they are caught, he thought, die and become reality. He touched her scared face, her dry black nose. Her soft ears and the hump of her silver back.

He lay down beside her because he could. He curled up next to her body, stiff under its fur. He had sensed she was tired and old. Snow slanted in the moonlight. He watched it fill the mouth of the cave. He could die if he wanted to, but he didn't, more than anything, he wanted to live.

He had his knife. He could make a fire. He had his camera. He brought the thick pad of her paw around his shoulder. She was as heavy as a nightmare. His head was against her throat, her chest and he imagined a heartbeat there, at last, he had her warmth. He picked some soil from her black claws and scratched it into his own fingernails.

He had food. She would feed him. His substance.

I'll be full of you when I come down off this mountain, he thought, and slept.

*

He can't remember the words his maman used, but words are mere exactitude, and it was apparent that during her sessions, the quiver around the letters was the frequency meant for the gods. So the sounds come to him, and because they are formless vibrations, they rattle him until his bones let loose and he shakes down to molecules, to dust.

It's just a body, son, she used to say.

"Dis moi ce que tu veux," she'd say. *Tell me what you want.*

"Maman parle aux dieux." *Momma speaks to the gods.*

And the sounds would begin. The tremors of candlelight combining atmospheres and unhinging realms.

"Vous ne pouvez pas revenir sur cette."

You can't come back from this.

It was true. He couldn't. There is a spell inside language that binds us to our ancestry, which has little to do with the words being said, rather the evocation of atmosphere sound provokes. Ordinary things, boiled cabbages and laundry days, when spoken in native tongue conjure landscapes and place and ghosts.

The dead live there.

And the people that we've been and killed to survive or willed to keep living. The dreams that manifested or died and the lies that truth revealed or buried. Laughter. Everyone's. What we remember isn't accurate because it's selected, but the way it shapes us is as real as anything we could touch.

Mathis thinks of this often and it's as though the different stages of himself were stacked and his mind, a borehole, tunnels through them all and his artwork, the echo through the tunnel.

Still.

He cannot speak of Callisto with a foreign tongue. She is native to him as though he was a terrain removed from the earth and singularly his own, without memory or place or utterance, unhuman yet human, like pre-birth. She runs up and down his tunnel.

Elle porte d'une dimension individuelle.

She bears a separate dimension.

*

The door had been left unlocked. He shoved it open, stepped into the house and inhaled an emptiness so thick it felt embraceable. He wrapped his mind around the knowledge that Nora was dead, that his son, Jacques, was gone, but alive. He walked to the window. Webs against his brutish hands and grime thick as snot on a tongue. He rubbed it against his sleeve, opened the view.

Jacques was out there. Dark green pines needled the clouds and bruised them like fruit. He knew Jacques wasn't dead. Knew it like a sleeping person knows when another was pressed against their back. That warm connection, he let it sink peace into his bones. My tired, dreaming bones, like old planks, he thought, turned and saw the encyclopedia open on the table.

Beside the red circle, lay the deeds to the house Jacques had bought. Mathis put his finger on the town Callisto. So this is how she'd return? He'd leave after he had rested. He'd follow his son. Track the bear.

31.

Callisto, Illinois

It was early morning when Mathis arrived. He'd walked all night along the river. His skin was sodden and his feet were wet wrinkled inside his boots. His son had not been difficult to track.

On the train he tried to think of something to say. Something that would bring the months back, but that which must be defended slips into insecurity, and Mathis was a stubborn man who wanted to believe in himself. There was nothing to photograph, so he whittled instead. And while he was carving a few words came to him, like a fleet of ships, they came and bashed against his sand in the shape of a poem.

He looked up at Jacques's house. The lights were out. He looked towards the garden. The sculptures lay before him like a mirage. They took his breath away. He walked through them. I'm inside a half-human game of chess, he thought, weaving in and out of the pieces, watching dew roll down their faces, their bodies, like tears. He helped one that had fallen to her feet. There was nothing skilled or smooth about Jacques's carvings. They looked painful and frenzied, like animal claws with human intention.

They looked like Nora. What had happened to Nora? Mathis knew that Jacques was trying to make peace with himself.

Mathis understood that monster. How it can rip out of you. He touched the sculptures, mournfully, as though they were victims, then left them and walked around to the front of the house.

The door was open and he stepped inside. There were two coffee cups on the table. He picked up a geode from a windowsill and walked upstairs. The only bedroom that wasn't empty had crumpled sheets. He touched the mattress and it was cold. From the window he watched the river. It was pewter colored and moved like a long jerking machine.

He walked down the stairs. His hand ran along the banister. There were little maple leaves carved into it as though it were a tunnel of wind. Jacques had chiseled maple leaves everywhere, on doorframes, window frames and baseboards as though he needed wind. Impermanence, thought Mathis, and touched a chord on the piano. The room pulsated the sound.

He took the carved figure he'd made of Callisto and twisted off her head. He took the poem from his breast pocket, rolled it up as small as a cigarette, pushed it into her hollow torso and popped her head back in place. She was the size of an arm and he stood her between the coffee cups.

He'll come back home when he's ready, he though, or perhaps he won't, perhaps he can't forgive me, but then, he thought of the encyclopedia laid out on the table. The map to Callisto, Illinois seemed to be proof that he hadn't given up. Mathis felt hopeful as he left, the air invigorated him and his steps were light as he walked to the road. He'd walk to town and inquire about renting a room. He didn't want Jacques to feel obliged to let him stay, as he knew their relationship was tenuous and would take time to heal.

A truck bumped down the path and kicked up dust. It stopped a few feet in front of him and he could see it was full of heavy men. Harold squeezed out from behind the wheel. His hat shaded his eyes and a rod of fear shot down Mathis's spine.

"Mr. Beaumont?" said.

"Yes."

"I see you've had a shave."

"Yes."

"Well," the man chuckled. "Now ain't that appropriate."

32

Harold walked back to the car. The window was rolled down, he leaned forward and placed his elbows on the door frame and spoke to the men.

"That's him," he said. "Let's get it done and dusted."

The men looked at one another, jumped out of the car and ran around to the trunk. Harold walked back to Mathis and grabbed him by his backpack.

"Get off! What the hell is this?!" Mathis struggled to break free.

"Only take a minute. Now hush," said Harold.

The men returned carrying tools and before Mathis could say or do anything a shovel smacked his temple. He saw a slit of weak blue, then his eyes, round as two worlds, closed.

"Take him down the road, boys. Not next to the car," said Harold and he followed as they dragged Mathis by the legs. "Here'll do," he said and they stopped and circled around Mathis.

Arlo parked his car a hundred feet down the road and walked towards the tools rising and falling. Small splats of blood flicked through the air like ladybirds. It was as though they were mining the body. As though they were searching for some wealth to keep. Some did. Some kept mementos. It's what the old timers used to do too. That wasn't so long ago. Arlo remembers clearing his Granddaddy's attic and unwrapping a foot, bone sawed at the ankle. His Father walked up behind him.

"Well I'll be goddammed, you know what that is? That's a hanging memento. They all did it. That ol' coot, keeping his handiwork after all these years. You go put that in the trash. It ain't a thing to have at your picnic," he let out a snort of laughter. "Now I shouldn't say that. Not these days. These days are different," he winked and ruffled Arlo's hair.

Arlo remembered light coming through the old slat boards and his Father's smile. Sure, some said he was crazy as bull in heat, but Arlo had always found him loving.

"Get me one of them fingers," Arlo shouted as soon as he was in earshot, his hands still resting in his pockets. He's a sentimental man. He looked towards the river at the distant tree copse were he had left Elora. Now why didn't he think to keep a bit of her before she got all bloated? Even though it chagrined his heart knowing she was with that nigger, even though, he knew he'd miss her little ways. Her eyes had been calf like. They'd been together years, not donkeys' years, but, hell, years all the same.

"Let's wrap it up now," Harold said and walked over to inspect. "Nice mince you got there," he said and threw them the burlap sack he'd taken from the trunk. "Fill her up," he said and walked over to join Arlo. "You gonna tell me what this is all about?"

"It's 'bout Elora," he spat chewing tobacco on the ground and didn't meet Harold's eyes. "Black bastard hurt her and it ain't a thing a man wants the courts to deal with," he said.

"Nope, not these days," Harold said.

"You got that right."

"And you got your justice," said Harold.

"I 'preciate it. And you know I owe you one, so."

"Yep, will do."

A few of the miners stuck bits of chipped bones like diamonds into their pockets. They took the shovel and scooped steaming piles of gravel and body into the sack. They strung up the sack and hung it from a tree. They wiped their hands on their wet jeans. They wiped their tools in the grass and kicked bits of gristle from the road where the animals could easily find them. They stood, catching their breath, under the hanging sack.

"Meant to have a heavy rain tonight," said Arlo. "It's good to get old-fashioned every once in a while," he patted the finger in his pocket. "Gives folks a sense of place. Now I don't need to tell you that this never happened. I may be the law, but I'm also just one man, and I thank you from the bottom of my heart. My Elora thanks you too. God rest her soul."

They all bowed their heads at the mention of her name. Above them clouds of red began to bloom across the sack. Arlo watched it with the serenity of one watching the sunrise.

33.

Elora woke. Mud and wet reeds against her face, green, brown, black, she breathed the violent, lung scraping breath of one cutting through the surface alive. But I am dead, she thought, for there was no feeling in her body, as though she'd been hammered out and cauterized by her own skin. Her body blackened without its rush of life and jetsam of fluids and dialogue. A dearth remained in a way that a canyon is still a living thing, but carved by forces now absence and from her canyoned mouth sounds lifted and fell, not like birds, but the idea of them collapsing midair and in pain. Her new form rose, disguised by the familiarity of her previous crust, but inside, she whistled with a clean emptiness and the only heat in her was the brilliance of memory. Hands.

It was the opposite of feeling. The opposite of being infested, but the swarming, the thronging inside the marrow was the same. A cut so deep it was numbing and her job was to realize the pain.

The river dried on her hair and skin. With each step, the ground crumpled, then rebuilt around her, as though she were walking on feathers, billows of white burst through the black, alive as any animal. Using her body was like being in a blizzard, for she had an idea of where things should be; houses, memory, people, thoughts, but her vision could only see white. She managed to stand, bones and muscles stacked into place. She walked through the white out. Beyond the whirling boundary, she could hear the mob of sculptures waiting for her to enter their domain. They knew she was blind and they scythed her with their stammers, hisses and wooden hands. She had received the life they had wanted. She ran past their groping towards Birdies and fell on the grass. The night was quiet in the way that prowling is quiet. She had to tell her body how to lift and move. The blood rushed to her ears, each beat of her heart was a collapse into her new skin.

This is me. I am this thing. Alive.

Nothing pronounceable would ever have meaning again.

*

It was as though Birdie had awoken to a blanket of snow. That quiet covering with a few scratches inside it magnified by silence. A knocking. A raccoon, she thought; no. Footsteps. Her mind, an unspooled cloth, quickly gathered itself to attention and waited. She could hear the snap of embers from the fire in the grate downstairs. She could hear a hand grab the bannister of her porch and climb the steps. She could hear the gentle knock on the door. It woke Franklin and the birds fluttered around the aviary.

"Who's there?" Franklin said.

Was it Arlo?

She rose and put on her dressing gown. In its pocket she placed the switch blade she kept in her bedside cabinet. The throat, she thought, if it's Arlo, I'll go for the throat. She knew she could not ordinarily outrun him, but was betting on the fact that he was blind drunk, so put on her shoes and grabbed her car keys. She opened the door and looked out into the darkness.

"Hello?"

She squinted, but could see nothing beyond a sky the color of old iron, ditches.

"Anyone there?" Birdie asked, but she knew the answer.

She felt could feel the presence of another stuck to her eyes like a cornea. Elora. The night was brimming with her, tidal with her. The darkness rearranged in greenish blue globules as though it were constructed of gelatin. Streamers of dull light and shadows rolled inside it.

"Elora?" She's out of my hands now, she thought, she's gone, just the spirit going to its house.

There was a puddle of river water on the porch. No, she thought, she's dead. She had seen her with her own two eyes. Hadn't she? There are many reasons for a porch to be wet, she thought to herself, closed the door and bolted the lock. Franklin flew to her shoulder.

You've had a fright, she rationalized to herself, everything is difficult and confusing right now. You've been injured and that's why you need to keep yourself together, you just keep yourself strong, Birdie lectured herself as she walked with Franklin up the stairs. He perched on the headboard and put his head under his wing for sleep.

"That's exactly what we need," she said to him, climbed under the covers and turned off her bedside light.

She lay there, eyes open in the darkness, something outside felt insoluble and not in a human, logical way. It encircled around the house like a memory. Nothing matters that isn't also invisible, Birdie thought and looked at the window. Love, belief, passion, death, dreams, hate: our lives are totems marked by invisible labors.

The curtains were pulled shut. She felt certain that someone stood behind them. Elora's blue watery face flashed before her. It took all of her courage to rise and walk to the window. Let's be done with it, she thought and quickly opened the curtains. Nothing, no face in the glass, just a small circle of condensation where one had been. She watched the breath vanish, but no one came.

*

Sleep came in fits. Birdie dreamed she had entered Jacques's garden. It was not dark enough. The firs serrated the sky. The stars were cold and lay across the river's long, broken sways. The back door was open and the kitchen light shone through in a long rectangle that lit up Jacques's statues. Birdie saw an ax stuck in one. She was too afraid to call out. There was the silence that falls after struggle.

She followed the flattened grass to the river and before she registered Elora's body, she stood confused at the water tapping against a still hand. In her dream, Birdie put her hand into the water and touched the fingertips of Elora, they moved. She grabbed the girl's arm and pulled her from the river. Elora vomited up water from her blue lips. She grunted like a heifer and the ground went warm and sticky.

The scene acquired her, dispelled her retina of its screams, and insulated her enough to be capable of action. She fell at Elora's side, her lips were still warm and a weak breath bubbled out of her mouth. Birdie caressed her forehead. There was blood everywhere, but mostly, Birdie noticed, on her legs.

A child, Birdie thought. "Forgive me," she whispered and opened Elora's legs. The baby's head was crowning. "Dear God," Birdie said. Elora drew a single, horrible breath and then her whole body contorted and pushed the baby into the river's mud and Birdie's waiting hands. It was not like any other infant Birdie had ever seen. Skin like the purse of a mermaid. Heart like the sharks shadow swimming within. Above her the stars rotated in a quick circuit.

What she held was not human.

34

The following morning Birdie went to Jacques's and found Elora sitting naked on the piano bench holding Mathis's carving of a bear in her hands. Her body was a translucent blue like a newborn chick's. The veins across her like cracks, bruises, like the inside of mussel shells and tight red strips that ticker-taped around her neck. She did not seem cold. Her eyes were filmy. Imagine seeds inside a watery pulp. She watched Birdie, and Birdie felt a rod of misery plunge into her and search her insides.

She's alive, but how?

Birdie sat down beside her and struck a key. She let the sound reverberate and expand into nothing before she hit another. Birdie felt the emptied sounds gathering in the corner like small beings, like spiders. They sat there releasing notes into Elora's vast anguish until Birdie spoke.

"How did you survive?"

Elora remained silent. She turned her head and looked out the window at the river. Birdie could not comprehend how Elora had lived. She had seen her float away. Hadn't she? When something happens outside of the mind's experience we pretend it doesn't exist or we rationalize it into something normal. She must have come up for air, Birdie rationalized. She must have caught on a log or something and floated above the water. All the same, Jacques's words haunted her.

I can bring her back. I have that power.

"You can't stay here," Birdie said. "I'll be back in a moment," she rose and walked up the stairs.

In Jacques's bedroom she found a sheet. She carried it down and wrapped it around Elora. Either way, she has beaten the odds, Birdie thought, and she needs me. Birdie looked closely at the small round of her stomach. Her skin was still gray from the water.

"You're with child," she said and Elora nodded.

"Come on," she said. "You're coming with me."

Birdie helped her to her feet.

"Help me through them," Elora said and closed her eyes.

"Through who?"

"Them," Elora pointed to the sculptures on the lawn. "They want me."

"Okay," said Birdie. "Okay, you've been traumatized, but we have that baby to think about now. That little one is our main concern. Come on, I got you," then Birdie lead Elora towards the yard.

Elora hobbled through the grass as though her legs were disjointed and held her hands against her ears. The world past her eyelids was florescent. The afternoon den of insects in the river's weeds. The suspicions of birds. The mind racked, like sheet metal music and the slow slew of sunlight against the sculptures as though each beam were a laser. She could hear them burning, that hot and disfiguring.

How could she live like this? How could she not?

Birdie led her up to the spare bedroom and tucked her into bed.

"He's done this to me," she said and Birdie removed a tendril of hair from her face and sat down beside her. Her mind was a dark station where memories of that night peeked around corners and through windows.

"I know, I know," she wasn't sure if she meant Arlo or Jacques. "But I'm here and you are staying with me. You're safe with me. No one knows you're here, so no one can hurt you. They, um, well, they all think you're dead."

"I'm not dead," she said. Jacques peeked through her mind's window, his white teeth, his hands. "Is he?"

Birdie took a deep breath. "The honest answer is that I don't know. I took him to the railroad station, but when I got back, Jimmy told me that Arlo had found him dead, which probably means that Arlo killed him," too, she stopped herself from saying, too, for the woman was here, right in front of her eyes, she was alive and talking.

"He knew. He must have. He knew they were coming for him and he carved this for me," she placed the wooden bear in Birdie's hands as though it were an infant. "Think of his garden," she said and in her mind Birdie saw red and yellow leaves cascading through woodenheads, wheaten light braided in the river.

"He created people," Elora said.

"Well, he certainly created one," said Birdie and looked at Elora's stomach.

"Tell me, when you took him to the station, did he mention me?"

"Yes," Birdie said, it was the question she dreaded. "He said to tell you to create something phenomenal, then find him. He said that is how you would recover. He wanted me to make sure you found him. He gave me this," she took his address from her shirt pocket.

"So he knew I would be alive," Elora said.

"Maybe. I can't make sense of it, but one thing is for certain, you have to let him go now. Arlo killed him, Elora, and if he finds out you're alive, he will kill you too. You have to think of your baby."

"Yes," she said and lay down on the pillow.

"That's it, sleep," said Birdie and she stroked the girl's hair.

While Elora was sleeping, Birdie performed a binding ceremony for the tiny carved woman. She cleansed a cloth in the river and wrapped it around the figure like a bandage, preventing the carving from causing more harm. She buried it in the ground before the first freeze.

35.

Birdie tended her. Every day she brought a spoon to her lips. It was only a small thing inside of an enormous one, a campfire inside a forest, but she tended her all the same, kept her spirit alive and burning.

But Elora was lost. For months, she believed in nothing but holes. Nothing was certain but the holes that woke her, that whistled her to sleep, until whole days became whole nights marking weeks, marking months where each one was indistinguishable from the next, which was the exact opposite of their beginning where every second glared against her like sunlight on metal.

She sat growing their child and remembering it all, his knuckle calluses, the pen in his shirt pocket, wood shavings stuck to his bare feet, a piece of loose hair on a plaid shirtsleeve. Arlo. Jacques had let her live, but killed her in the process. She was unable to feel, and could only observe each dazzling trace of her past life, as they spilled into one another, grinding away, gnawing away at her heart like acid, a billion microscopic mouths working, working her back to nothing. Teeth.

*

The winter was mild and Birdie was thankful. She cooked for Elora, kept her warm and gave her clothes to fit her growing stomach. Snow fell and melted over Jacques's wooden army. The whole scandal became folklore and Arlo, "poor Arlo" he was now called, had a freezer full of casseroles. Birdie said nothing. She seethed in her torment. The anger in her crashed like thunder in a jar. Elora also said nothing. She didn't speak. She just ate when Birdie made her and lay in bed. At last, when her belly was swollen enough to pop, she broke her silence.

"Bury them," she said to Birdie. "His women. I can't have them out there. Speaking to me, calling for me, please, just get rid of them."

It was the end of May, the baby was due any day now and Birdie was nearly seventy years old. How could she bury an army of women?

She rang Stan and asked him to come with his son, Stan Jr. and a shovel. She was making his favorite rhubarb pie when she heard their motorcycles chop up the path and park outside her house. She walked out on to the porch drying her hands on a dishtowel, while he took off his helmet and smiled at her.

"Your undertakers have arrived, madam," he shouted up to her.

"Thanks for coming," she said and he gave her a big bear hug.

"It's not often you ask for something," he held her shoulders and studied her, judging his next remark and decided she needed a bit of normality. "We can talk later. Look at you. Jesus Christ, woman, you just keep gettin' better lookin.' Listen, you ready to make an honest man outta me yet?"

"Hell no, you wouldn't love me half as much."

"Shiiiit, I'd love you double," he said and she snorted.

"He won't be able to get down on one knee much longer you know," Stan Jr. said as he approached them. "Hey, Birdie."

"Hey darlin'. You're all handsome and buff. Get over here and give me a cuddle," she grabbed him by the neck, pulled him close and the three of them squashed into one another.

"He's right! I'm an old codger now, my sweet parakeet, just say yes and let me die happy," Stan stroked her hair. She pushed his hand away.

"Shut up, come in, sit down and have some pie."

"See? By God, it's like we're married already."

*

"Why don't we drift them down the Missis? Let her polish them back to something decent," Stan Jr. said putting his clean pie plate in the sink. "It near breaks my heart to see trunks all cut up like that. Burying them would be difficult, plus it seems a bit cruel, you know, a trench of bodies in the ground."

"That sounds like a good and soothing idea," said Birdie.

They worked the following night, releasing each one into the black river like a silver fish. Birdie thought of Elora rolling down the river, saw her snag and catch on the debris, saw her hair billow underwater like some soft tentacled urchin attached to a pale rock. She sat down on the grass. Her whole body was outlined in sweat and her insides were full of mucus. Stan sat down beside her, she hadn't told him what this was all about, but he understood that she only kept secrets for a good reason.

"This feels crazy, Bird. You ready to talk about it yet?" he said.

"Yes, but I can't," she let her head fall against his shoulder.

"I see. You know, parakeet, you look tired. Why don't you come back to the city with us for a while? Huh? No questions asked," he put his arm around her shoulders.

"I'd love to Stan, but, again, I can't."

"Come on. It'd be good for you. Get the brawl in your blood. We'll listen to music. We'll dance and eat ribs."

"Honestly, I can't. I'm looking after a girl. She needs me. That's why we are getting rid of these sculptures. They bother her."

"No kiddin'? What's she got that I don't?" He nudged her side.

"A baby in her belly."

"Damn, she has me there."

"Only in event and not in looks," Birdie laughed and rubbed his enormous Buddha belly.

"Oh yeah? Well I'm working on the perfect 7lb 5oz little shit in here for us, woman! It takes time and dedication to make a love baby," he said and massaged the sides of his stomach.

"Oh Christ. Jr. help me up lovely boy before I drown in your father's bullshit," she put her arms out into the air and Stan Jr. lifted her gently. "Thank you, my dear."

"Now that's the fightin' Bird I like to see," Stan rose with stiff effort. "How many of these broads do we have left? Let's get the job done," he said, picked up a sculpture and carried her to the shore. "Off you go, my beauty."

They worked in silence, slipping them into the water, and when they were finished, they stood watching them bob up and down like a fleet of wrecked figureheads, rolling, rolling back to the sea.

*

Elora lay in bed and listened. She could hear them speaking, Birdie and the two men, but more than that, she could hear the sculptures release themselves like burning coals to the water, there was relief as their murmuring stopped. She imagined their bodies eroding back to nothing, their cuts smooth and worn away until they were unrecognizable.

On the nightstand the carved image of a bear looked over at her peacefully. He'd left it on the table as a gift. He had told her that his Father had tracked and photographed a single bear for twenty years. Callisto was his obsession. Perhaps that's what the carving meant? Perhaps he was telling her that she had become his animal? I am, she thought, I am his obsession. He can't be dead. He will find me again, she thought, and the first wave of pain hit, she screamed like she belonged to it, wanted it.

She heard feet running up the stairs.

She sat on the edge of the bed. Still. Her heart hung from her ribcage like a single talon holds a falcon to a cliff. The voice was a whistle that rolled through a canyon; a hiss. The voice distant and muffled. *Elora, Elora.* A scream underwater. *Can you hear me? It's Birdie.* A scream inside a gloved hand.

She touched her arm, skin on skin like red steel on a pale petal, *Elora.* Her voice breaks through. *Elora, the baby is coming.* A siren. So loud it blurred.

36.

The pain left her breathless. The sheets were wet and she imagined the water soaking though the bed. It calmed her, she took little breaths, saw the water spilling through the floorboards and the downstairs ceiling, leaking through the living room, the basement, past the cracks in the cement and into the deep tissue of soil. It soaked all the way to the center of the earth where it began to boil.

She heard boiling. Sheets ripping. She breathed into the sounds and the pain traveled through her and broke like bubbles through the searing. Birdie was there. Her voice was a smooth chant, but there are no words for life pushing through you, no words for the beginning of life.

There is air only, breath only, and the awe at what we are up against. It is stunning that humans have survived despite such traumatic and frail beginnings. Tiny beings of instinct, little sensory organs, sprinting out towards the light, she flew like a wet bird, a girl. We are a hungry species, from the second we are born, we spend our lives wanting and needing nourishment, changing only what feeds us. Our hunger is desperate.

*

She was stillborn. Her name was Lorelei Beaumont.

Clouds layered the sun. It glowed like a white mouth through muslin.

That was just it. She was still born.

He used to use an imaginary chisel and cut into her body. He told her he was leaving his design. That's what he's done, Elora thought, he's turned me. Into something lifeless of his own making.

It was as though she had aborted a dream she'd once had, and it changed her, how could it not? She had carried death inside of her body and through the sheer force of will, had released its form, but not all of it. Part of it stayed with her, as though her cave had been a room their child had smudged its handprints across, death had left its imprint and for a while it looked as though Elora, or whoever she'd become, was never coming back.

All dreams are placed somewhere, in love, in action, in drink, in seas of regret, she built hers like a stone tower around herself, and from the top, she watched. In waiting, she placed her dreams in waiting for the return of feeling. There was nothing and everything that she wanted.

And so the absence of life became one.

37.

Elora sat in the chair and watched the prairie, the river. All day, every day. All week, every week. She could see the exact spot where they had buried the child. The small, perfect mound of earth and imagined herself trading places with her daughter. Imagined herself as a curled fetus in the tall grass, red, raw and infected. It seemed so desperate and extreme. Imagining herself this way had an intrusive violence to it, as though she were a stranger standing in the shadow of a lit house. The allure of the ugly and disapproved. In her mind she gently poked this image of herself with a stick like she would an injured animal.

If Jacques were still alive and she found him, could he bring Lorelei back? A child without sensation is no child at all. Her grief was a feeling that took place outside of her current body and inside the memory of her former self. She knew to grieve, but felt no pang of emotion, and it was the sense of nothingness that kept her a nonbeing. To not exist, yet to have a memory of the way one exists, requires a torturous adjustment. What would a child resurrected into oblivion eventually become?

What had she become?

With an examining reverence she considered the way the earth re-digests itself. The methods of disease and infestation the earth had created to re-digest us, to change the form of our bodies, our minds.

And, perhaps, our souls.

She considered the things that burrow and eat flesh and the ways to hollow a person, to decompose a psyche, decompose a body, so that it returns to the earth to feed what is new. She is new. Somewhere, her child is new. There is something so gorgeously economical, gorgeously practical, about the way each thing dies, even a mind, after it leaves, still eats from somewhere, feeds something. We consume ourselves and through our demise we make way for something better, greater, so that nothing is ultimately wasted.

But time.

It passed and she filled it with the pictures of herself, that she cut from scratch after scratch and rip until she was sure she couldn't feel it anymore. Until she was sure that she'd begun building some sort of clockwork heart to claim. One that might grow and function.

*

"She stares," Birdie said to Stan.

He rang to see how Birdie and her lodger were coping.

"Stares at what?"

"Anything and everything, she just stares, and stares and doesn't speak," said Birdie.

"Best get her a camera then," said Stan, always practical.

"A camera for what?"

"People need to find a reason for odd behavior," said Stan. "That girl needs to be around people. She needs to see there is life out there, ready for the plucking, and there is no place so full of life as Chicago. But we can't have her walking around the city staring at everybody like a damn zombie, can we? Get her a camera, get her used to it and get her up here."

"Stan, you are a genius."

*

Birdie went out and bought her a Kodak Retina "1" Type 118 camera that afternoon. She placed the camera on the armrest of Elora's chair.

"If you're gonna stare, use this," she said as she sat down beside her.

Elora looked up. It was true. Apart of her adjustment meant that her ability to concentrate had changed, as though she could see things that others could not, which made her stare openly at the world. Well, the world outside her window.

"I figured you needed tools. Like a mask," Birdie said.

It could have been anything. A violin. Knitting needles. Binoculars. But a camera seemed the perfect accompaniment to her stare.

"I can't sing," Elora said. "I've tried and I can't."

"Because it sounds bad or because you haven't the heart to?"

"Both," said Elora.

This mouth is not my mouth. This tongue is not my tongue. These vocal cords are not mine, yet I belong to them.

"Well, I'm sorry about that. I know you loved singing, but there are many ways to release. Use this camera as a temporary release. Just until you get your voice back," Birdie said.

"I won't get my voice back," Elora said. "This is my voice now."

"Well," said Birdie as she patted Elora's shoulder. "You can do the singing yourself or you can make things sing," she got up and went into the kitchen.

Elora took the camera in her hands and held it up like a weapon, a gun.

*

Jacques had once showed her a photograph his Father had taken of an osprey. The bird dipped into a slim rift beside the ocean and was slanted with its wings fully spread. The camera angle was perfect and portrayed the bird as a bridge with one wingtip appearing to touch the cliff edge, the other, a wave, fixed and breaking all at once.

"Look here," Jacques had said and pointed to what looked like a smudge.

"What is that?"

"It's the reason I love this photograph. Look closely."

"A shadow?"

"Yes, another bird's shadow. See the spread of wings? It can't be the same bird."

"I do, that's amazing," she traced her finger over the imprint.

"You never know what you'll capture when you cut a slice of time."

*

The following morning Elora woke up and walked outside with her camera. The first snow of the season was wet and sluiced the morning. The river diminished inside the white and Jacques had been gone for months, for a lifetime, forever, an hour.

In her hands she held a machine. It wasn't so dissimilar to herself. It could lay up the images of time, but could not live it.

She heard a gunshot, hid behind a tree and saw, ten feet in front of her, a goose fall heavy as a weight from the sky. Its wings were still spread in flight, its neck was twisted, its wet eyes were black and its beak was open in shock. Blood poured from its upper chest.

Right away she saw the potential and used her foot to move the red into a circular pattern so that it resembled a sun with splattered rays setting into the feathered head.

Seconds after she'd taken the photograph, a dog arrived, snatched up the bird with its spitty jaws, then disappeared, tail wagging, over the hill. She looked down at the stain the blood had left in the snow and saw more shapes in it, a mask, a rose.

Death is when a thing changes shape, she thought. That is all.

She stared at it for a long while without feeling anything and imagined herself as a bird locked in a block of ice. A small body locked in a dead cold, blue and foggy, with only a pair of black eyes looking out, unblinking and afraid of overheating, of melting and releasing a tiny bird's frantic heart.

*

Birdie had built her a small darkroom in the closet of the spare room. She gave Elora an egg timer, a thermometer and a book that described how to mix the chemicals and unload the canister onto the reel. Elora practiced each step in the light a dozen times before she felt comfortable attempting to do the same in the dark. When she turned out the lights, her other senses took over, and she found that her hands, though unsteady at first, eventually understood how to work the equipment. Once the lid of the developing tank was secure and the chemicals were at the correct temperature, she started pouring the mixtures into the tank and timing her agitations on the film. She rinsed the chemicals from the film for ten minutes, then holding her breath, unscrewed the developing tank and unrolled a row of ghosts.

The perfect imperfection. The film hadn't completely developed and had a granular washed-out effect. Dark blood pockmarked the snow. The goose's body appeared weightless against the white, as though it could be brushed away, only the blood showed gravity. It was exactly what she wanted to capture. A way to mark time as manufactured by her, staged by her. The camera was a box of emotions that didn't require a claim.

She started orchestrating her photographs. It gave her control, as though she were designing a montage of deliberate representation. It also acted as a reference library for feeling. The goose on the snow explains how the brutality of survival can diminish light. She could rationalize this as truth, but could not experience it as emotion, like a mirror she had began to see herself through the lens.

Her orchestrations themselves were small still lives. The parts of recent activity that represented vanishing. Birdie's reading glasses left on the table and shot throughout the day at different intervals, so the thin wire shadows suggested time. Discarded shoes. Open drawers. A hand towel with wet patches on it. A pile of cut fingernails. Like a study of the mundane and routine, but inside each photo, she placed the small, thumb-sized paper crane, as a way to honor the goose.

Its grounding had given her flight.

It made absolute sense of her being, for up until that point, before and after the river, she had been parading herself as real. She walked and breathed and made all the correct sounds, but always, her internal rhythm was a beat off, a pulse late, deeper, sonorous. She was the echo that bounced off her loss and along her days. But the camera was her own timepiece, no chance circumstance, no misgivings, the shutter snap was the second between her sound and the outside.

She used the lens to capture her subject's interior through her eyes as though she were a conductor, and similar to water conducting electricity, it gave her a surge. In the way that singing once gave her a surge. She was not an ocean, a river or a stream. But more like a photographic lake, inert and unmoving, a reflection of what a human should be. Somewhere along the line, her stillness was replaced by a numbness that's remained frozen for a long time. When she skates along her photographic history she always arrives at the goose. A strange thing to spark the light of consciousness. As strange as a fire inside an igloo and as life preserving.

It was a way to live.

38.

Birdie had been at the shops. When she arrived home that afternoon she had found the front door slightly open. A heat was coming from inside where Elora sat meticulously cutting out the pages of a bible with an Exacto knife.

A book on origami lay open by her side and she was folding an army of scripted animals that she hung, one by one, from the room's ceiling with string and masking tape. Crease, turn, crease, turn, crease, paper punch hole, tie string, stand on chair and hang. It was a slow process, a methodical process that left her entranced and exuberant.

"What in the world are you doing?" Birdie asked as she hung up her coat. She stuck a lump of fired chicken wrapped in foil in the refrigerator.

"Can't you tell?" Elora looked up in surprise. "I'm creating a fortress." Her eyes were arrested with shine and Birdie knew she'd tipped off-balance again.

Birdie slumped down in the chair beside the fire. She felt tired and weary and unable to cope with another one of Elora's bizarre episodes. She had learned to keep her heart out of such behavior and play along.

"What kind of a fortress?"

"A stronghold. It's for our own protection."

"Protection from what?"

"You never know. But first I'm going to secure the ceiling in the living room, then the kitchen and my bedrooms. Is that the right order?"

"I'm sure it is. Chicken's in the fridge if you get hungry," she got up and went upstairs to have a bath.

It was difficult sharing her space with someone after all these years of living alone, especially someone that was crazy and possibly, even, undead. Over the months she has often spoken of moving in with Stan, but Elora refuses to leave the child's grave and Birdie doesn't push the matter. It was fine as long as she could keep Elora hidden. At the moment that didn't seem to be much of a problem as only Jimmy visited her. There was a myth developing around Jacques old house and people kept their distance.

By the time Birdie had finished her bath, Elora had folded and transformed religion into wilderness, into wings and fangs and freedom, so that an overhead jungle of biblical defense swayed from every room in the house.

Elora was lying on her back beside the fire photographing her floating zoo. She put the camera down when she saw Birdie.

"Soldiers can be so beautiful," she said.

She watched her creations hang in their suspended universe, each one, a still little death. She heard the scotch tape give way and saw a paper crane drop to the floor.

Birdie opened the bird and read its stomach.

"He shall tear it open by the wings, not severing it completely, and then the priest shall burn it on the wood that is on the fire on the altar. It is a burnt offering, an offering made by fire, an aroma pleasing to the LORD." Leviticus 1:17.

Birdie stood in the doorway. "That's enough," she said and began opening windows. With a frosty roar their bodies rustled and cracked at the wind's touch, paper wings hit paper paws smacked paper necks, twisting and struggling, harnessed and caught.

Birdie grabbed a broom and with sweeping arm movements, mowed through the lettered animals. Their delicate bodies tore and fell in pieces to the floor.

Fell around Elora. She did not rush to save them, instead, laid expressionless as Birdie cleared each room, sweeping bundle after bundle into the fire without her protest. The flames rose with hot ferocity and when she had finished, Elora sat by the hearth and watched the fire eat. The hairs on her cheeks, her eyelids, reddened and singed, her skin was hot, yet she stayed, watching through the unforgiving night and into the morning long after the embers had turned black and gone cold.

Birdie slept on the sofa that night and in the morning found Elora still on the floor. Her hair hung in sweaty coils down her back, a brown wool blanket wrapped around her boney shoulders. Defeated, deflated, a cavity, a stone cellar caving in. Heartache throttled the throat of her dejection. She was skin disguising a worm-infested fruit, heartache had eaten through her, and in her hands she held the smudged paper crane. She was rubbing it between her forefinger and thumb. She didn't look at Birdie. She stared at the cold coals.

"They were clouds on the ceiling. You burnt the clouds," she said, took her camera and photographed the embers.

39

The "crane incident," as Birdie likes to refer to it, broke the back of Elora's silent mourning. She went around stomping and smacking her limbs as though she hadn't felt them before, as though she were beating the life back into herself. She spent hours arranging rocks, thimbles, hairs plucked from her head, screws, orange peels and anything else she could find to pattern into a still life. A small table in front of her window was the stage for her photoscapes. Once they were arranged, she would wait patiently for the perfect shadows to appear, then press the shutter down.

Jimmy delivered a large box of film and chemicals. Birdie was happy to keep Elora supplied with photography materials, as strange as her themes were, they seemed to be healing her. At least she was talking now, Birdie thought as she opened the door for Jimmy. Elora was upstairs with the window open, hoping for the winter wind to ruffle the feathers she was attempting to photograph. Hearing his voice sent a wave of repulsion through her.

"You some kind of photographer now or somethin'," Jimmy said to Birdie.

"More of a somethin' but I try. Call it my retirement hobby. I could show you some pictures if you like?" She wouldn't have asked if she thought he'd oblige. There was no way he'd step foot inside a witch's house.

"Nah, not my thing. Say, you hear about that nigger's old place?"

"You mean Jacques? Doesn't it belong to his family?"

"The man's dead, Birdie. You think his French relatives wanna come out here? Their lawyer says he can fix up some deeds owing to the extenuating circumstances and all. These lawyers can do anything. Some poor s.o.b. from Kentucky bought it," he said.

"Why?" Birdie stuttered.

"Exactly my thought, but I guess it was too cheap to resist, though who the hell knows. I just hope it's not another troublemaker. This town's had its fair share of trouble and it's good to get things back to normal," he said.

"Whatever normal means," Birdie snorted.

"I've never been confused about normal. Nope, and I don't know many folks that are. Maybe you're the only one that's confused about normal round here," he said and got into his truck.

"You're not wrong," Birdie said. "So when are they moving in?"

"Postal redirection starts next week, so soon, real soon," he said and drove away.

Elora had been listening. Someone was moving into Jacques's house. *That nigger's old place*, they couldn't even bring themselves to say his name. Nigger is a terrible, grisly word that demands excuse. Initially it was the sting of hearing this word rather than its actual intention that surprised her. Its crash in the air like air followed by a bang, the sound but not the intent that caught her. That's how they saw him. That's all they saw. A story about a dead nigger, not a name, not a man, a lover, a creator.

She sat on the floor holding the carved bear. She could almost feel him alive and something else. There had to be another explanation, she wanted a reason to justify the look of distance she often saw in his eyes, not a look of malice exactly, but the remote coldness of one who has been left behind, back-wood eyes, she thought, wasteland eyes. They shared this now. She realized it was a way of feeling. They both shared the unforgiving gaze of the exiled; a bloodline burned by circumstance that left a smell about the place like hair burning against hide. She caught this scent, like a hunter, she smelled their hearts, flayed victims, the pungent meat of terrible love and prejudice. The unknown truth was a rope that bound them together and at the same time pulled them apart; it was a noose.

She placed the bear in the middle of the feathers, waited for the wind and took the photograph.

40

"Meatloaf tonight," Birdie shouted up the stairs with more enthusiasm than she felt. "Come on out," she said. "You're not going to make me climb the stairs for nothing are you? Come on now, honey, I know you're still alive because you ate the sandwich I left you."

No answer. Dammit all to hell, Birdie thought as she climbed the stairs, she's probably in there holding that bear.

"She says she's feeling him, feeling Jacques, that she's feeling he's alive, like a goddam diving rod or something," she'd told Stan during a recent phone conversation. "It is enough to break your heart. She spent months sitting in that chair, staring towards the field where her baby was buried. Remember the little thing, terrible, like a stone with a skin covering. Poor, desperate girl, she cried so hard the world cracked and dropped her into the pit of herself, but now, shit, she's nuts. I'm all for creative madness, you know me, but she's screwing screws into mud pies and photographing them with that bear and an origami crane. Now what on earth is that about?"

Birdie knocked on Elora's door.

"Can I come in?"

"Yes," Elora said. She was still wearing her unwashed dressing gown.

"Christ, you look like a ghost," Birdie put her arm around Elora's shoulders. "And smell like a dog."

"I've been working," Elora explained.

Birdie looked at Elora's table full of mud and objects. Feathers were poked into the mud so that they stood upright and the bear was positioned behind them as if he were peeking behind trees. Birdie sighed. Symbols, it all boiled down to symbols, sometimes she knew what they meant, other times they were obscure. Elora's belonged to the obscure camp, but at least she was using them.

"Take my hand," Birdie said and led her to the bathroom. "Have a shower and then come down for some meatloaf. It will do you wonders."

Elora entered the kitchen soap fresh from her shower. Her shampoo mixed with the smell of onions and garlic.

"I started sautéing without you. Here, sit down and dice this pepper," she told Elora and began rummaging through the cupboards for flour and spices.

"Good," Birdie said. "Now put everything in this bowl and squeeze the mince between your fingers until it's blended. Therapeutic isn't it?"

They molded the meat into a bread pan and placed it inside the oven. The methodology behind cooking had always eased Birdie, focusing on the sequence of one ingredient following another until reaching a stage of completion, plus it brought a bit of order into the house. They sat down at the kitchen table and began chopping up the remaining vegetables. After a while, Elora stopped and cleared her throat.

"I can't let anyone move into Jacques's house," she said. "It should be mine."

"That's difficult because, technically, you're dead."

"But I'm not!"

"Yes, we've established that. We've also established that if you show yourself as living, you will certainly be killed, again," Birdie said.

Birdie clasped and unclasped her hands, making her veins pop out and flatten again. The poignancy of baking onions and garlic made her eyes water.

"I'm sorry. I don't mean to be crass, I know I've said it a thousand times, but it's tragic how life can chop into a young tree. A person needs time to grow a history. Give yourself that time. There is nothing to do about the sale of that house. It's just a thing."

"The piano is in there," she said.

"That piano was there when he arrived, but if it means that much to you, photograph it," Birdie said.

"I can't live like this. I can't."

"You can and you will. You already are," she put her hand on Elora's. "Listen to me. It's awful that life struck you before you had the chance to thicken, but flesh grows around the axe, Elora, until the axe becomes inseparable from the tree. This will become you. It will never leave, but you will heal around it and to heal you need to turn it into something, something you can stand to look at, whatever that might be. Jacques was right, don't you see? You need to create yourself again."

"I am creating myself again! I'm taking loads of photographs! I rarely go outside in case I'm seen, I'm stuck in here, like some crazy woman. I think I am some crazy woman," Elora said.

The idea for her gallery came to her then, as perfect picture and already developed. A gallery of emotions like a reference library, she saw frames with staged faces, she saw herself.

"We need to leave. Before the house is sold," Birdie said.

"I'm not sure I can," Elora said.

"I know it's hard," said Birdie. "Hard to let go. You both resembled the world in your own special way, had that in common, saw things with an artist's eye and there is no sick like lovesick, but you are wasting yourself here, wasting away. There is no need for it. You could start again."

"There is nowhere to go."

"You are young. There is everywhere to go, but start with Chicago, I could get you a job there, nothing fancy, but it would pay the bills and get you out of the house, out of here."

"I don't even know where I'd begin."

"I'd help you. You know I would," she got up and put her arms around Elora's shoulders. "The trick is to only love the things that love you back, that's it, that's the trick for relationships, friendships, work, hobbies, everything. Think about leaving."

41.

She can still remember how the wheaten sun had pressed the afternoon into his bedroom like steam. She had come in the morning and lay on his bare chest. He slept. She listened to the culvert of his body reverberating and his breath. So much was working beyond her control. She felt waterlogged and swung her wooden legs out of the wet sheet, then rolled off the bed like a tree off a cliff, boom, she crashed and moved towards the hallway's cave, shadowed and fresh, cold hands on her shoulders, cold breath coiled around her neck like an eel of white air.

There was the sensation of sinking as she made her way to the bathroom, splashed water on her face. The hand towel smelled of damp dust, outside the air was ready to cook; through the window she could see leaves hanging from branches, gray inside the house's shadow. The sun, a giant leech, sucked the blood from everything.

She poured two glasses of water and went back to bed. He was just waking up and she handed him a glass of water.

"Thank you," he said and plumped the pillows up behind himself.

She placed her glass on the bedside cabinet.

"I heard you were in town the other day," she said.

"I needed some things."

"You could have asked," she said.

"I didn't think I needed permission to buy toilet paper."

"CC said you were bold, that was his word, *bold*," she underlined an imaginary word in the air. "Arlo told me."

"CC was an ass."

"*Bold, ass*," she underlined two words.

"It's not like I lied about going," he said.

"Lying and hiding the truth are the same things, Jacques."

"I hate it when people use my name to make a point. Fine. You are right, Elora. I kept it from you. I lied. We all lie."

"How am I lying? I just want to know if you are going into town, so I can prepare myself when Arlo mentions your name."

"You're lying because you're hiding your truth: me. I'm stuck out here like some stallion lover," he said.

"Oh for Christ's sake. You *are* bold. Don't you know anything? You're out here to keep safe. You were crazy to move here in the first place and you're even crazier to stay."

"Maybe I'll leave then."

"Don't let me stop you and certainly don't let me take advantage of you," she rolled her eyes.

He put his hand on her stomach and stuck his finger inside her bellybutton. "You can take advantage of me," he said.

"Get off."

He turned over and pulled her to him. "I don't want to argue. Something's changing."

"What do you mean?"

"I'm not sure. It's strange, but I feel like we're waiting. I keep hearing this sound, this music, when I'm working. It's synonymous with you." He kissed her hair.

"What do I sound like?"

"Let me listen," he put his ear against her forehead, adjusted her nose like a dial. "Ah there it is, seagulls."

"There are no seagulls in Illinois."

"Trapped seagulls then."

"I have something for you," she said. She got up, went to her satchel hanging on the bedroom door handle, and pulled out a small cigar box. "It's not for you exactly. Inside are my most precious possessions. I would like you to keep a hold of it for me, you know, in case Arlo does find out. In case something happens."

42

Elora has pictured the evening of the fire a thousand times. It was the first real day of spring. A dry winter had waned and left the fields a brown, dehydrated flat, but the air was warm enough for birds. The whippoorwill's song had already begun.

The seagulls were circling. All night they had called her, roused her from her bed, and she watched them from the window. They dipped and skimmed the river and perched on Jacques's eaves. The spread of their wings, bright white against the off-white sky, like sheaves of paper with written messages she could not decipher.

They were from him. She dressed, stuffed her camera, Callisto, a candle and matches into a satchel and walked out the door. Birdie kept a gallon of gasoline in the garage. Elora picked it up and entered Jacques's house.

The piano stood in the corner like a living beast. The rustle of a hundred seagull wings and feet meant the roof felt alive. She moved the piano into the center of the room where the lit rectangles from the windows joined. She placed Callisto on top of the piano's lid and set up the photograph. She sat on the windowsill. The shadow of her body fell across the dusty lid. In the center of her outline stood Callisto. She sat still, photographing the light as it moved through the morning and afternoon like a sundial, circling Callisto, reshaping shapes, reshaping her.

Birdie came and stood at the door, nodded, then walked away.

When the photo was finished, Elora went upstairs to Jacques's bedroom and retrieved her cigar box from underneath the bed. She put the box and a towel from the bathroom in her satchel, and then soaked the bed with gas. Then she poured gas all the way down the stairs, circled the piano, splattered the drapes, emptied the rest on Jacques's chair and lit the candle. Dusk was hours away and the sun was behind the house. The living room was cold and the candle splayed a golden circle on the piano's lid. Callisto stood behind it and she took the final photograph of the house's interior and placed Callisto inside her satchel.

She stood with the candle at the window and placed her palm on its glass, then dropped the candle in the seat of his chair and left the room. Behind her she heard the fire crack, like an old door opening, she walked down the porch steps. She needed air, distance, and scope.

Across the yard, a low beam of sun caught the tin watering can and filled her eye. She turned away, the air was cool on her cheek, and then it was gone.

The air was still, so still it polished trees, the dark shed.

Dry grass broke underfoot, crunched like a shelled bug, she walked. She could feel the hard knots of earth underneath her feet, like jutting bones poking the undersides of her boots. Her feet slid inside her sweat. Her whole body had begun to sweat. She wanted to be clean, baptized. Behind her she could hear the house burning.

She ran until she hit the road and the sharp grind of gravel, then she stopped, dust whirled around her, collected on her swelling tongue, soaked the wet from her eyes, pores. She turned off the road and entered the prairie's hiss where the grasses rubbed against one another like a crowd of hands planning something sinister. A cloud of gnats rose from its soggy bottom and with them the smell of decay, she heard small animals dart out of her way.

She moved through the prairie until she reached the creek. Roots from a few pine trees bent towards the shallow water as it twisted along its pebble and mud bank. Their shadows encased the pungency of pine and turned earth. The pines broke up an otherwise overcast blue sky, they needled the blue, needles spiked the blue, and she was thankful, for the sky was too big to look at, an echoing, sorrowful melancholy that fell too low and reached too far in every direction. So she followed the creek, carefully stepping over anthills and hedge balls, sticks dipped and raced on the shallow water's spine, minnows and frantic water beetles nipped from tiny inlets where the water pooled a murky brown. She walked slowly, she cultivated solitude and after a while the birds resumed their singing.

She followed the creek all the way to the pond and stopped on a flat dried patch of mud around which tufts of sickly grass were trying to grow. She undressed and walked towards the pond. The mud cracked all the way to the water's edge, where she stood, as if she had reached the end of a map and had to step off into murky oblivion. She entered the water up to her neck. It was as brown as dark chocolate, though not at all silky, as there was a cool fine grit to its ripples. Pebbles lodged and dislodged between her toes, then she lifted her feet and did the breast stroke. Water bugs skipped out of her way, her head was constantly parting a cloud of hoverflies, her foot scraped against something hard, possibly the shell of a snapping turtle. She turned to look back at a row of snapping turtles sunning themselves on a nearby log.

You can scare yourself silly swimming in a pond, a reed gently brushing against your leg can easily be exaggerated into a snake, a leaf clinging to your stomach becomes a leech. She had come here before, always when she on the edge teetering; the dark water challenged her body to reconnect with her mind. The dark water forced reason to emerge. She was not a strong swimmer, so it was necessary that she eased into herself and relaxed in order to remain afloat and usually this trick worked. In the early days of her Father's illness, miscarriage and Arlo, she'd come here when she didn't have wounds the water could infect.

Her heart had refused to slow despite her rhythmic and steady breathing. She swam until she was too exhausted to continue, then wrapped herself in her towel and sat on the bank. She could feel a thin residue of mud drying on her skin, later it would brush from her arms like salt. She sat on the cracked ground and pulled her dress over her head, the dress clung to her damp patches of skin. She untangled her hair with her fingers, lay on her back and fanned her hair across the ground to dry. Her hair soon felt and crunched like black straw, her heart beat quickly. In her mind played a succession of small bells, she thought of nothing, yet could not sit still, so continued walking along the creek.

She saw the chimney stack first, an unsupportable presence hovering in the air. She stepped away from the creek and out into the prairie to have a better look. A large oak hid the shape of the house, but the chimney stack was unmistakable, a brick finger pointing up.

The house had silvered from the wind's touch, a smooth bone. It's back half had collapsed so that when you looked through the front door you saw the sky, splintered gray bones and rusty nails were weed-gripped and scattered across the ground. There was no sign of glass as sparrows flew in and out of windows and eaves were stuffed with nests. Weeds sprung up through cracks and holes in the porch. As she approached, she heard a steady drone and saw, in the corner, an enormous hornets' nest, like a clay tornado plastered to the wall.

She stepped back and turned towards the tree. A barely visible fence had long ago broken under the weight of brambles, red stalks and green leafy heads of rhubarb were scattered across the yard like giant spiders, and patches of green onions sprouted over mounds. She sat down facing the house. The sun was beginning to set, its golden head was framed by the door and the house beamed with a rich internal light. Everything blackened against its gleam. Shadowed birds dipped in and out of golden pools and a breeze blew shadowed grasses and shadowed branches, hornets like black dots pinged inside the gold. Even Elora became a black mound that sharpened against the gold until the gold began to burn out, handing the world's details back to her softened by twilight. With full eyes she watched the sun melt through a magenta sky, thick as a garment from which clouds, like plums, hung.

Overhead a flock of seagulls flew north. She knew the house had burnt to the ground.

43.

Imagining herself starting the fire is now like reassembling a dream, blindness then fuzzy images, a glimpse caught in a mirror or a shop window, how you can look vaguely familiar to yourself, a nose, cheekbones, parts you recognize as your own, but then a certain slope of the neck, the way the eye is caught, something new, alien, what you do not know but adorn. His face, a reflection in the water, the form of a child, waiting. Jump, he says, jump. She remembers that there was an emotion that she waded through, as if hanging from a shaft of atmosphere.

The fuming heat. The blinding sunset. A resigned evening. As if whatever change had occurred had been completely accepted by the twilight, almost casual, yes, the world seemed casual, suspiciously casual. She noticed no strain, but for a few tense stars dimly shining through the heat like small hearts trying to beat on the outside. It made them seem violent. Violent because of their delicacy. Brooches of light pinned to a pink neck strung with crimson, violent. Doves locked in a hot cave. No not that, rather the eyes of trapped doves glaring through a hot cave and out into a blackening night.

You see, even though she had yet to understand how the world hints, she remembers taking notice of those stars, which is why she must recall them exactly. Even though she did not heed their warning, instead left them, barely flickering, too pale to shine and penetrate her thick chest of understanding, even so, they caught her attention. Then nothing seemed as important as living membrane thin against the earth and open. How else? How else to receive clues? Look. The clues are everywhere.

*

She followed the creek back to the house, the roots were more twisted than she had remembered, so she had to plan where she placed each foot. The trees shadows were thicker, the mud thicker, mosquitoes whizzed small jet songs past her ears, the sound of crickets turned the darkness into a single animal. She could hear the earth opening its pores to the night's cool touch, she loved the solitude, she accepted the night, welcomed the night. She ate the night. She ate and ate until she was only night covered with a transparent skin; to look inside of her one would see stars. She was nobody. Not even rabbits seemed shocked to see her.

She couldn't take in exactly what she'd done. Alteration is as simple as a flick. The mind allows only what it believes the body is capable of managing, it is a censor with the ability to disconnect, to foresee, predict, conclude, long before the body realizes how it has changed, why it has changed. Then it filters out our lives and gives it to us in chunks small enough to swallow.

She saw the hill glowing, then the fire whipping out and up through his house with orange arms, red arms and black bursts of kicking. It was kicking. It was pounding.

Birdie came running across the field, shouting indecipherable words. Birdie grabbed her and held her close, sobbing.

"It's over now," she told Birdie. "It's all over."

Something died and this was just the finale, the sacrificial burning of a body, hollowed and done.

*

A heart does not admit, cannot dismiss what is seen, could never say that stars do not exist, that what is seen is a remainder, a bright remnant of light, left, left burning a dark sky, left to prove a body of fire that once existed, that had died, too soon, perhaps, so that it decided to leave a bit of its presence behind: a flicker, a lantern, the lighted window of a distant house, as if to say, I was here, I was here. What we wish upon is only a memory, what we wish upon is gone.

*

Without speaking they watched. The smoke burned the back of their throats, they were too close, yet could not move. Their eyelashes, their cheeks seared, yet they did not blink, could not blink, could only stare and stare at the flames arching uniformly towards the sky. A raging tulip, beating, eating, disintegrating the house back to nothing.

When the fire brigade arrived, the house was mere embers. Birdie saw them charging through the field.

"Get in the house and hide!" she pushed Elora through the door and shouted to the fire brigade. "Leave me! I wasn't inside, I'm not hurt, go away!"

They put out the fire, Elora watched from the window, but she does not remember seeing any water. Only the smoke, billowing, billowing smoke, clouds of smoke, mountains. The moon was high in the sky. Seen through the smoke the moon grew small, so small it became a pupil and the sky was an eye that glared at her.

A weak star, that's what her child was like, she was like, no, not stars, but constellations. Untouchable because they had been punished, burnt out.

She had found a way to own her body, celestial or not, she took up her camera and photographed the burning house. With the camera in her hands, she had found a way to feel.

44

What happened inside Elora when she started the fire:

Listen. I asked myself a couple of questions. What is death? The sacrifice of a body. What is life? The sacrifice of a body. And love? The sacrifice of a body. The answers are all the same. Then there was a battle. How could I fear what had always been present? Loss has been present, has constantly grown inside of me, silently as hair, as fingernails. It has grown so long that I can feel it snarl, scratch and cut.

I can hear it. The seagulls. Were his. How do I make this skin mine?

I sound very similar to coyotes. Every evening I wait for them to come close. They use the field the child lives in to scope for prey. They paw, back and forth, the night. Out of the window the sun is low and I hear them coming.
The ground beating underfoot.

My heart. It is true, true –
My heart has not allowed his words.

His yes or no.

My heart has not allowed false words.

They took him, her, they took them away, beating underfoot, beating.

And he made me again. I drip them into my black dollop, fill it like an empty sack. They drip into my black. Pit. Fall. Hit and fall through my black, black. Where song once hid.

They took the song, all of it. Now.

This tongue is a dead snail. A locked flower. A fist that cannot open.

But it is not silent. What I mean my body infers:

Look at me, moving from ice to fire. It is the moving that matters.

The photographs like an ice covering.

Beneath my ice, a river of shiver, I shiver and bones. As if they were full of cracks. Underneath my surface I see his face. My face. Frozen. Icy eyebrows like white splinters. Her small human shape. His mouth echoes my name. Erodes the blue flesh preserving me. Thaw, he says, thaw, she says.

And then. A flame. A way to extinguish.

The enchantment before the burn. Fire melt me.

The burning escape. To drip until I run, my wax dreams run. We run. It is what humans do. They ran him and he keeps running.

There are places where he feels alive, brings life, can bring her back and in them, in me, an army gathers drive.

I point my finger towards the disease. Prepare to attack this disease, I say. Here. It flicks in the eye's corner.

      Red. Red. Watch him go.

I run with my body as a shield. Towards victory.

There are horse clouds alongside me,

alongside the blue,

bugs fly out of the grass like rockets

and the coyote in my chest howls as though it's cheering.

Everything is red rimmed, meat around an eye and him running.

Underfoot, they beat.

Pound through the timber. Snap twigs, stamp mud.

Pound through the prairie. Break stalk, bend grass.

They howl. They howl like someone wanting out.

In need of a place to enter. In need of a place to exit. The answers are the same, remember?

I light a candle. I wait by the window. Come here. This way.

I speak to who I am now. This is the way. In the window my golden face quivers just beneath a black pool. It does not look like me at all. But another woman, a watery glow, a light behind muslin. She reaches her hand towards mine. Our fingertips touch cool glass. Why have I not seen her before? Beautiful, muted, a bubble rises from her lips. A reflection. A photograph.

The candle on the curtains, the candle's in his chair.

And the fire crawling like red spiders crawling across the wall,

      like blood spilling,

            soaking up through the curtains,

               like an idea –

the idea that it could die,

           all of it, could die and live again.

I let the fire burn.

Without the fire she would have vanished. Our fingers were touching. The glass was so cool between our fingers. Together we slowly placed our palms against the window.

I set the house on fire.

so that the part of me hanging,

the only part of my life,

of my person that the world could see,

the disgusting bit that hung,

limp and oily like fatty gristle from the meat of my soul,

could sizzle, writhe, wilt and die. I want to be. Again.

Quiet. Quiet. So quiet that birds land on me.

45.

The morning sun rose as the bust of a dead fish floats to the surface of a still pond. Ash, ash, ash like silver fish scales coated everything, her face, leaves, grass, bushes, the river's edge. Ash collected in droplets of dew before running in clear lines down the shed. Pale bronze in the morning sun, it was early, the moon still bold in the sky, the clouds thin in the brown sky like white plastic bags floating beneath a watery surface. Elora walked to the pile of smoking wood, wind blew the ash in visible currents down the hill and above the prairie, they were being scattered, thrown, given back. Using a stick she searched through scarce remains. Like an insect on bone, looking for things to keep, a way to digest what had happened, meat, anything, anything to sustain her.

She grabbed a gardening spade and walked to the grave of their child.

She dug a small hole, placed a blue cornflower inside it and filled the rest with ash taken from where Jacques's house once stood. Fire, they say, replenishes the earth for re-growth, yet there was nothing left, save a suffocating flower.

She has thought about this, about flowers and what they need, about sun, and about soil and about rain, stems, and petals. How we exchange breath with plants and how, we, too, shrivel without sunlight, and hide in winter. How our hair can be the color of a marigold, a hyacinth, our skin, pale to the shade of hibiscus, or dark as bark and orchids, our lips, when pressed, become the tight folds of an unopened rose. How we can die screaming, but without a voice.

It is how they killed him. How they were killing her.

She has seen this, she has seen unnamed, undocumented, unborn flowers in the eyes of the silenced, their eyes and their pupils like seeds. Their fingers, roots, reaching in the dark, waiting, her child and countless quiet ones before her fertilizing the ground with their bodies, for others to plant in.

She did not want to recite verse or sing. She just stood, listening, for a long time. She listened as far as she could until she could hear the drone of silence. Goodbye, she said to the silence, goodbye. Goodbye. Then she started walking. Birdie was waiting in the car.

46.

Chicago, Illinois 1955

After the fire she took a fresh look at herself and what she saw there she kept hidden. Birdie got her a job as a waitress at Stan's diner and moved her into an apartment in Lincoln Park.

She thought she needed to be around people. In the beginning, she'd stand in the center of a busy sidewalk and let the people cut around her like a tide, people splashed against her, people roared at her and tried to pull her down. The people were angry. She put her arms out, she wanted to touch them as they passed, to contact anger, to let her own anger out; she did it to feel. The people stormed and crashed into her, they bruised her, but it was just the thing she needed; a good long scream.

Thank you, she said to the people, I hate you, I love you.

After that, she climbed to the top of her stairwell and out onto the flat black roof of her apartment building where brick chimneys stood in a thick collection of bird crap like tall red trees with white flowers growing at their bases. The buildings reminded her of gray stalagmites; all around her drains dripped, gray water swirled into gutters, down pipes and calcified crevices as if the city was melting. She pretended to be a bat hanging from the top of a cave looking down at the cement stalagmites.

Spring stretched into summer and still, each morning, she returned to the roof where the clouds hung in the low, gritty heat. On the street below the pigeons cooed and picked through garbage bins with mangled, broken feet and she'd crouch there, watching them, blowing into her coffee cup, waiting to hear the footsteps of the first morning commuter. Usually it was the same blonde woman, whose passing caused the pigeons to flare up and flap like a quite applause.   Eventually more people began to trickle down the sidewalk. Two people walking side by side, two here, one there, a handful of people, multiplying until their footsteps became one giant footstep and the street was full. Pigeons dove in and out of the crowd.

The people moved like a shoal of fish and the pigeons were pushed to the side or suffered broken toes. The people were in unison but remained unattached, only the birds communicated, cried their small warning cries. After a while she felt the need to nullify and disappear inside human cohesion. So she stopped climbing to the roof of her building and learned to walk a city street, shoulders square, quick paces, head down.

She knew nobody. Not really. Nobody knew her.

That's the way she wanted it and for a while it worked, but Stan's small and friendly diner was not the type of place where you could remain invisible.

*

Having the loss of Jacques and her child was like having a cat in a bag at the bottom of herself. It was there kicking and gasping, yet she knew she needed to let it die, so trained her brain to shove it down and press and press it into the deep excess of her mind. But always she thought of it, carried its claws, she dreamed it awake and dreamed it asleep, as though her juice, her acid, had liquefied the creature and it had become her and she'd sink into the details.

A whippoorwill, an eyelash seen and then blown from a fingertip, rain on tin, wood and rivers. All these little details, glistened like sweat on skin, were the exterior and did not represent the whole. The whole was something else. Something she couldn't make out, but felt huge and unimaginable, a beast, and her person was simply the wind its thrashing disturbed.

The photographs helped. While taking the photographs she hovered in the balsam-like wilderness between sleep and coherence where the mind exchanges dreams for reality.

She tied her dressing gown around her waist and walked into the kitchen. Coffee. Coffee monster, black river of sanity. Last night had been difficult and long.

She lived in a one-bedroom apartment on the third story of a redbrick building. The walls were white and covered with her photographs. Her bed was in the living room because she used her bedroom as a darkroom and studio.

Apart from a few kitchen essentials and a round wooden table with two chairs, there was little else. She loved the apartment because of the tall window that overlooked a canopy of beech trees planted in a row alongside the pavement. Stan normally rented it out to students and she was lucky that it was empty when Birdie drove her to Chicago. To decorate she pushed the table in front of the window and bought a geranium in a terracotta pot. That was five months ago. Starting a new life was challenging.

The sound of children was a surprise, like a good omen, she thought, that's what children should be. She hadn't even realized there was a school across the street until the new year began. That's how preoccupied she'd been with forgetting where she'd come from. She struggled to release her past. Every day she had to push memories out of her head like steering a cloud of hysterical bats through a hole the size of an eye socket. It was difficult and exhausting and some days, some nights were better than others.

She looked at the empty bottle of wine and single glass posed like conscience on the countertop. She knew she'd been drinking too much lately, but it seemed the only way to deaden her dreams. She had frequent nightmares, where she felt like she was drowning in the river, where she feared Arlo was close. She dreamed of wooden women and hands around her neck.

Last night she was lucky. The thought had left as quickly as it had come, as if it were a red ribbon of ticker tape that she had to pull from her mind until it ran out and plunked her fears down like shiny pennies on the table. Where she could see what they cost her.

Last night's heat was stifling. Her body had searched for coolness. She pressed her cheek against the white wall and opened the window. The smell of hot asphalt was a gel through which sounds dropped like bricks through the night's air: a motorcycle's engine, a car horn, a dog's bark. Sound was a rock in her throat. Was this anxiety?

She felt the urge to flee, so grabbed her keys, her camera and walked into the street. There had been a short burst of rain and a moon floated inside each puddle like a white petal in a fishbowl. She took a photograph. A police car sped past; its blue siren was a frantic bird flapping against the sky, her chest. She watched a street of watery moons shake.

She walked to the river and stood expectantly at the bridge. She put both hands on its cement railing, leaned over and breathed in the deep water. It smelled muddy and sour, even putrid, but she needed to see natural movement, she needed to see something flow its natural course. She looked up. The moon was low and hanging between two buildings like a silver portal that extended its rippled arrow, its path across the river towards her. She felt as though she could jump into the moon, become a myth, retold, reinvented and time enhanced. She looked down at the water and saw her reflection, like a trembling black thumb that white shards of light lapped against, then closed her eyes, two moons burning through her pupils and out the back of her skull like headlights.

She clicked the shutter down and captured herself, again and again, until she made it through.

47.

Apart from her own shadow, she resisted photographing living forms and concentrated on movement instead. The empty carriages of the L, the waves of Lake Michigan, flags, trucks.

Her ongoing series titled Hanging Smoke, where she suspended a black metal hanger with fishing line attached to a curtain pole. She dangled the hanger above the chimney stacks and waited for the smoke to curl around the shoulders of the hanger like a bolero, a dress, a scarf, a necklace. Ghosts. When she developed the photos she could see the current of a person inside the space, arms, neck, chin, because that's what her mind expected of the view. And when that happens, when we see only what we expect, truth becomes its own deception.

All the while, something was waiting inside of her like larvae underground, every photo she took felt like the process of scratching out, where she was becoming stronger and stronger, until finally, her gift was revealed. She didn't notice her transformation at first.

One of Elora's neighbors kept homing pigeons on the rooftop. Elora was eating a sandwich and waiting for the furnace to release its steam around her wire hanger, when the neighbor asked her to photograph his birds. She took a bit of bread and fed it to them as she circled the pigeon loft and photographed them preening. They had just returned from a flight and each cubby hole was full.

"Stand next to them," she said to the neighbor, but he declined.

She took a single group shot of the birds before she heard the furnace kick on and release its steam across the shoulders of her hanger.

In the evening, as she was developing the film in her darkroom, she could hear the birds plucking seed from the rooftop. It was distracting and as she dipped the paper into the chemicals she beckoned the birds to be quiet, then clipped their photo up to dry.

A cry reverberated from the pigeon loft and she ran up the fire escape. Her neighbor stood helpless with his head in his hands, a few birds lay lifeless at his feet. Elora looked inside the loft and saw the other birds dead inside their nests.

"What happened?"

"They just died," he said. "All at once. They dropped dead, as if their hearts stopped beating at exactly the same second."

She knew she had silenced them.

The following day she walked to the pet store and bought two mice in separate cages. She had three pictures left on the roll of film inside her camera. They rattled inside their cages on the kitchen countertop. She photographed the brown mouse once and the white mouse twice.

Inside her darkroom she tried to clear her mind and think of nothing as she shook the developing tank. She sat in the dark and waited for the chemicals to activate. Show me who I am, she asked. I want to know who I have become. When the timer rang, she opened the tank and cut the film. She submerged the photo of the brown mouse into the solution and summoned it to die. She sank one of the white mouse's photographs into the dish and bid it to live. Then she clipped the photos onto the string and studied them. There was no difference between the two. The brown mouse's photo hadn't begun to fade or change in any visible way, as she imagined it might do, yet when she left her darkroom and entered the kitchen, the brown mouse was dead in his cage. The white mouse, however, was scurrying along happily.

"I'm sorry little one," she touched the white mouse's cage. "Don't take it personally."

Back in her darkroom, she dipped the second photo of the white mouse into the developing solution and told it to die.

In the kitchen the mouse lay in a ball of white fluff, still warm, but completely dead. Awestruck, she removed the two mice from their cages and laid them out on the table. On their backs with their paws touching as though they were brothers. Their small stomach's were still soft and white. The light from the extractor fan was artificial and perfect. She reloaded her camera and took a single photo, then scooped the mice into the trashcan.

There was no remorse to feel.

This was her true nature.

And the world that she had once been a victim of, now seemed as vulnerable as a small throat inside her clutch. She could make the ultimate decision. Power was the first feeling to come back to her. This must be how Jacques feels; she thought and remembered the words he had whispered to her. *Now, we can both escape.*

It wasn't the existence she expected, but she had certainly escaped, and now that she was beginning to understand her new ability, she felt responsible for providing a particular type of justice.

She had a reason to live.

48

The first human ritual she performed was on a man she met at the diner. It was an accident and she can't remember his name, so titled his photograph Penicillin, which seemed appropriate as he started out as bacteria but strangely ended up as a healing remedy.

He had the mouth of someone who had smoked for a long time. When she turned to get his coffee she feared he might pinch her bottom. His laugh was obnoxious and practiced. He took up a four-person table for two hours during the lunch rush. He only drank coffee with free refills. His eyes followed her wherever she went.

"Pathetic. Fucking pathetic," Ros, the other waitress, said as she placed an order. "I mean, he's not even hiding the fact that he's mentally undressing you. Seriously you should get Stan to walk you home tonight."

"I doubt he's dangerous," Elora said, and he certainly can't kill me, she thought.

"You never know. He gives me the creeps."

"Humm. Maybe I will speak to Stan," she said.

"Did I hear my name? 27 cheese steak and fries is up. That's you, Ros," he handed her the plate and turned to Elora.   "What's up?" He flipped a burger.

"That guy over there," she nodded in Penicillin's direction.

"What's he doing?"

"Touching me with his eyeballs."

"Ah. Here's 28 burger, jack cheese and no pickle. Want me to fix him?"

"Nah. I have a better idea. Can I take Smith for a walk this evening?"

"You bet," he said and tipped his chef's hat.

Stan had had two Rottweiler's. One named Smith and one named Wesson. Wesson had died a year ago and Stan had her tattooed across his back so that her muzzle reached up and licked his ear. Since Wesson died Stan brings Smith to work. She hung out in the back alley and waited for scraps. Stan brought her in after closing time when he did the paperwork. It curbs her loneliness, he says. Smith was loving and gentle until she heard the words "sic'em" and then she became a malevolent force of muscle and jaw. The diner had been robbed a couple of times and Birdie worried about him.

Stan and Birdie go way back. Stan was in love with Birdie. Said she was the only person he'd actually marry. He called her Parakeet or My Formica because she was classic, colorful and solid all at the same time. She called him Foolish: the best name for her was the one she already got. Birdie had spoken to Elora briefly about their relationship on the drive to Chicago. They had been lovers, long ago, when he lived in the desert. He once wrote her a poem that compared her to a flowering cactus. She kept it in a box with seashells glued in patterns all over it.

"He's gentle," Birdie had said, "and he's a tribesman. That's why he'll scarify until he finds a home, an identity worthy of his tribal heart. I am a nomad. I know where I belong. But I visit him. Like a cloud. I grace the old hills of his body whenever I breeze into town," she said with a grin.

It was a month of pleading before Stan let Elora photograph him. She'd found the perfect chair at an estate sale. It was an old powder blue dental chair. The chair of a chieftain. At the same sale she found a taxidermy barn owl. She made Stan a crown of knives and syringes glued to a child's bicycle tire. He refused to wear a loin cloth but agreed to wear his apron. She spray-painted the owl gold and glued it to the top of the chair like a mascot. Smith and Wesson sat obediently on either side of him and he used their head as armrests.

Elora used India ink to circle sun rays around his eyes and on his forehead she drew the winged V of a bird. She rubbed oil along his tattooed arms and legs until they shined. He sat straight backed in the chair in boxer shorts and greasy apron with his feet shoulder width apart and looked every inch a chieftain. Don't smile, she said to him, but his eyes couldn't help it. The photo hangs in her studio gallery. It has a gilt frame. Nobility. Chief Stan it's titled. It hangs next to the photo of the homing pigeons.

When she developed the photo of Stan she begged it to live, live, live and he had. In fact, he admitted he had never felt better.

She had been looking for someone to relieve the world from and Penicillin seemed like the perfect person to experiment on. She couldn't risk Arlo seeing her without being absolutely sure that she could dispatch him. She had dreams where Arlo was holding her under the river and she couldn't reach her camera.

After the last customer left, she and Ros wiped down the tables, washed the dishes and counted the tips.

"Ego the Romeo left you something," said Ros. She took two beers from the cooler and sat down in the booth across from Elora. Elora looked up.

"What? Money? Jewels? Keys?"

"Nada. Behold, the Business Card of Bullshit," Ros said and flicked it on the table along with Elora's beer.

"None for me, thanks," Elora pushed the beer away.

"Are you serious? You just worked a double?"

"I'm cutting down. I don't like my fuzzy head."

"Fair enough. Your sainthood is my gain. Can you believe that's all he left?"

"Who?"

"Romeo. Hello. I cleared his table. After two hours, he leaves a business card."

"I know. I really want to photograph him. He's unbelievable."

"*He's* unbelievable? You're unbelievable! Why would you want to photograph him?"

"When will I get another chance to capture an asshole?"

"Ummm. At the Hand and Spear every single Friday. Besides it sounds dangerous."

"I have a plan."

"Shit. Here we go."

"It's perfectly safe so don't look at me like that with your funky eyebrows of disapproval. I'm purely taking Smitty for a walk."

"A walk?"

"Yeah."

"How do you know you'll find him?"

"He kept asking me where I lived. He asked me if that was my blue bicycle parked outside. He touched my hand when I was refilling his coffee, said 'you didn't jump. I like that.' So I'm pretty certain he'll be out there," she said.

"Be careful. Call me when you get home."

"Okay. Don't worry," she stood up to leave.

"I hate artists."

"I know you do," Elora said. "Bye."

49.

She grabbed her coat from its peg and swung her camera around her neck. She knocked on Stan's office door. If you could call a larger than average broom closet an office. He was hunkered over his books and chewing his tongue. A green desk lamp was on a small table.

"God, I wish I still smoked," he said and glanced up at her.

"You look like Mr. Scrooge."

"Mr. Scrooge is the taxman, not me. I just want to feed people," he put down his pencil. He had a goatee like a small upside-down fire on his chin.

"So more of a Jesus figure then," she smiled.

"Pah!" He spat in surprise. "Yeah, that's me. Jesus. Let me show you what I can do with a fish," he laughed.

"I'll pass. Listen, can I still take Smitty for a wander?"

"You bet. Lead's on the peg. I'll be here for another hour or so."

"Okay. See ya," she said and he grunted a goodbye.

She walked up the stairs and went out the back door.

"Smitty, here honey," she handed the dog a half-eaten burger she'd saved in a napkin and attached her lead to her collar.

From the alley you could see the bike rack on the sidewalk under a streetlight. Sure enough he was out there, leaning against the light with his foot on her wheel. He hadn't seen her yet. She walked down the length of the alleyway. He heard her footsteps and turned. A huge grin slashed across his face. Then he saw Smith.

Elora bent down and unattached Smitty's lead.

"Sic'em," she said to the dog and the dog leapt like a snarling, barking bullet.

The arrogance in Romeo's face dropped like a curtain and terror reigned. That was the first photo Elora took. Within seconds, Smitty had him pinned to the ground and was rag-dolling his jacket. The shots she got of him pleading were the best. The one she chose to hang in her studio gallery was of him shielding his face with his hands. The streetlight makes his skin drop off below the cheekbone. Only one eye is visible and it juts out, huge as a bouncy ball. His ear looks like a wet slug. A grilled street drain shines under his head and his defending sleeve is torn.

That was right before Smitty broke skin and Elora called her off. It took a while to attach the lead. Romeo jumped up, scrambled and ran away. Smitty calmed down and eventually looked around, tail wagging, like nothing had happened. Nobody had passed. The street was still a street, and yet, she'd done something to transform it. She felt wild and impervious. There was no sign of the kicking bag in her stomach.

"Good girl. Now let's go for that walk," she scratched Smitty behind the ears and Smitty shook and splattered the drool from her muzzle.

Elora walked exuberantly into the night. She was high as a kite. She loved to capture a person's visceral. It was a powerful feeling. The power of one who breaks the lamp and captures the genie.

That night she developed the photos. Each time she agitated the tank, she remembered his face, his arrogance. He reminded her of Arlo and she wanted him dead.

In the morning she walked to the diner for breakfast. An ambulance and police cars were parked outside.

"What's happened?" She asked a newsagent.

"They found a stiff by the bicycle rack," the newsagent said. "Apparently he was attacked by stray dog and had a heart attack. It was a lucky break as the police have been after him," said the newsagent.

"For what?"

"The officer wouldn't say," he said, "so, you know, it's serious, hell, one less criminal nut job in the Windy City is a blessing."

Now she knew it was absolutely not a coincidence. She knew that having had Jacques inside her, having carried his child, meant that she had resurrected inside his realm.

The cat in its bag kicked all the way to the surface.

Kicked her throat.

What had she done? She had taken a life.

And why didn't she care?

She started running. She sprinted all the way back to her apartment and up the stairs where she closed the door and locked the dead bolt. The only sound in the room was her loud breathing. She stood staring at a windowed square of sunlight pooling across the floor. It almost reached the opposite wall. She didn't want to walk through it, so she sat down on the floor and waited for the cat to stop banging.

The only way to truly understand and, therefore, control her ability was to try it on herself.

Could she die?

50.

Her memory was full of images, each one hung like a dress from a clothesline that stretched endlessly over the contours of her mind. At any time she can walk up, choose a dress and put it on. It plays around her body like a mist. Stepping in and out of her history like this keeps her separate from it, keeps it from becoming skin.

The images of her past life hung alongside her current life. She toured through herself when she walked around her gallery. She was everywhere, yet, she was missing. There wasn't a single aspect of her existence that she had chosen. Photographing herself felt like an opportunity to own her new life.

She waited for inspiration to come and when it did it came from an ordinary thing like it usually does.

The neighbor's cat had left a rabbit's kidney on their doormat. Elora didn't think they would mind if she collected it, so scooped it up on the back of an unopened electricity bill. It reminded her of a fetus. She left it on the countertop, grabbed a plastic bag and walked outside to find some grass.

She took a black top hat down from a shelf in her wardrobe, and then glued tiny mirrored stars all over its crown. She placed the grass in the dip at the top and laid the rabbit's kidney inside of it. She put the hat on her head so that it completely shadowed her face. So that the viewer recognized the hat was inhabited only after close inspection, and she took the photograph.

She didn't know if she'd choose life or death when she developed the photographs of herself. She had killed and felt shock, then comfort, not repentance. Her old self recognized this behavior as psychopathic and wrong. Her old self thought that perhaps she ought to be released from her being, so it surprised her when she chose life, resounding life, as she dipped the negatives into the solution.

"It is decided. This is the life I choose," she said. "So be it."

It wasn't one that her Father or Arlo or Jacques had chosen. It was hers and she saw her photographs for what they were.

Her photographs had been surges of emotion that merely reflected an intensity she could not stir in herself. It was as though time had lacquered her and circumstance had soaked its stain into her bones. Her subjects were strikes against her rigidity. That's what she was building, creating, a tool to use to stab a haemorrhage. Would she ever be anything other than cold? And did it matter really, so long as the record of feeling was there? Of course it mattered. She wanted to be a better person. An artist.

And the thing sacrificed again and again? Love. And its various coats. Sex, passion, longing, patience, obsession, she drew them to her just to slay them away.

It was around this time that Gilbert appeared and she realized that she had the ability to feel guilt.

51.

Gilbert came regularly during a month of morning shifts. Stan had nicknamed him Mr. Clockwork. After a few weeks of sunny side up and strawberry jam, he unexpectedly took her hand.

"I'd like to introduce myself," he said.

"Go on then," she said and snatched her hand away.

"I'm Gilbert," he said.

She felt a flair of disappointment as the name wasn't definitive enough for her love. It hung in the air like a limp banner.

"Hello, Gilbert," she made her voice snap at the 't' and it sounded like she was scolding him.

He smiled. "Can I take you out for lunch?"

They sat in the park eating sandwiches. He was an art student and reminded her of some noble painting of a skinny boy with shoulder length wavy hair, wearing brocade and posing with a terrier. He had the aristocracy and thinness of regality. She was always asking him if he was cold. The dark colors he wore made him appear sickly and he curled into her like a child. It was obvious that she'd break his heart. It was her intention. She needed obsessive love in her gallery, someone as infatuated as she had been, before she contacted Jacques. Breaking Gilbert's heart would protect her. He was the only relationship she had after Jacques, and after a while it became clear to her that she was just using him to test her level of control. She should have ended it then, but she needed to know how her gift worked. She was just waiting for the means of the photograph to expose itself, which it eventually did. In a thrift store window she saw a pair of gothic candlesticks. She bought them and rang Gilbert that night. They had been dating for a few weeks.

"Gill," she called him. "Come now. I need you," she said and hung up the phone.

She felt like the harlot of some horrid movie, but set about preparing the room anyway. It was dusk and there was a train in the distance. It made her think of things far away and moving from her uncontrollably. She took out a pen from a drawer and wrote the word 'uncontrollable' on a piece of paper. Pigeons were cooing and flapping their wings like a signal from the otherworld.

She pushed open the window and leaned outside, arching her back like a figurehead. She could see him at the top of the street. She could tell it was Gilbert because he moved lithely. Lithely, she said to herself and went into her black room to light a circle of candles. She took her shirt off. She had on a Pendelton Turnabout skirt with blue cranes all over it. Her bra was standard and white and she tossed it on the floor. She heard him coming up the stairs and her stomach lurched. With her camera around her neck she opened the door.

Her saw her and stopped, stunned, she grabbed him, pulled him close, kissed him and wrapped her legs around his waist. He groaned and buried his head in her neck. He smelled like a damp city. She took him into her black room and sat him down in the middle of the candles. She straddled him, his leather jacket was cold against her chest and she shivered while she kissed his large Adam's apple and all the way up to his small lips. His mouth tasted of sleep and his hair was rumpled.

"Gilbert," she spoke into his mouth, kissed his top lip and he hummed in answer.

He traced the outline of her shoulder blades and ran his fingers up and down her spine. She put her finger on the shutter of her camera like a trigger.

"Gilbert," she breathed into his mouth like an incantation. "I can't see you anymore. It's over," she leaned back and the flash blinded him for a moment.

She quickly stood and started taking rapid pictures. He went from broken to baffled to angry in seconds. She circled him taking pictures. He stood up and looked around at the other photographs pulsing in the shadows like people in an audience. It dawned on him that he'd been set up.

"You bitch," he said in a whisper. "You organized this? You did this? What are you?"

How could she answer that? A nonbeing?

He was too shocked to shout. The darkness, the constant flash, the candles and the faces of her other photographs had stunned him. He opened the door and the severe light of the corridor made him furious. He started kicking the wall.

"Good," she said. "That's good," as though she were instructing a model.

She circled around him taking photographs; she was fearless, as though the camera were a shield. When his anger wore out, he lumped in the corner near the scuffmarks his shoe made on the white wall and started to cry. Excellent, she thought and continued snapping the shutter. He looked up at her incredulously, stood and walked down the stairs.

She immediately began to develop the photos she'd taken of him. She willed him to live as she agitated the developing tank. She instilled strength in him as she dipped each photo into the solution. Would it work even though her subconscious found him weak and annoying?

In the morning she found a note slipped under her door. 'Rot in hell,' it read. With relief, she attached it to the last photograph with a safety pin. She made a movie reel of photos beginning with the first and ending with Gilbert walking down the stairwell. Around the frame she glued ticket stubs.

She felt a small amount of guilt because she understood his pain, but he would recover, and now she knew for certain that the willpower to override obsessive love was in her image armory.

It was time to find Jacques.

They used to play this game.

"Hold out your arm, palm up, and close your eyes," Jacques would say. Then he'd softly move his finger from Elora's palm up to her armpit.

"Say 'now' when you think my finger has reached the inside of your elbow," he said. When Elora shouted 'now', his finger stop and she would open her eyes to find it far from her inner elbow.

"Let your skin be sensitive," Jacques would say, "you need to soften." He'd shake Elora's arm, "soften and receive things."

Elora lay on her back and raised her arms into the air. She gently stroked them one at a time. "Now, now," she'd say aloud as she passed her inner elbow. Her skin was so thin that she could see two thick purple veins running from wrist to elbow. She stopped stroking, placed her right forefinger on the thickest artery and waited to feel her heartbeat.

You're alive, she said, I'm coming.

*

To leave a place is simply to turn direction, for it only feels as if we are moving forward because of our relationship with time, but often we leave in order to reenter the past and attempt to correct it. The mind knows no difference; the mind is a compass needle that points in the direction of growth. To reach him she will follow the river.

*

She was due some vacation time, but Stan still wasn't happy about her decision to take it right away. She didn't want to explain that she was going to find Jacques because she knew that Stan would tell Birdie. She wanted this secret all to herself. Ros took the majority of her shifts and promised to water her geranium.

She packed her artwork between blankets inside the trunk of the car. She had rented a Buick Skylark, just like Birdies. It would be less conspicuous when she drove into Callisto.

All of her clothes fitted in a single suitcase. The cigar box was underneath the bed. It was black and the size of a book. It wasn't heavy; she could hold it with one hand. She'd always kept pieces of herself inside it like flowers pressed in a dictionary: that delicate. Like the little abbreviated notes people make to themselves: that personal. Like the leftover shapes of a cut paper snowflake: that random.

The carving of Callisto was inside the box.

When Elora first arrived in the city she dumped the contents of the box onto the bed and ran her hands over them for the first time since the river. The objects seemed to belong to a different person. Touching them seemed to initiate a need to do something destructive and fierce. She began jumping up and down on the bed as hard and as high as she could, knees to chest, then slamming her feet against the mattress. The bedsprings barked like beaten seals. The relics crashed against the sheets like wreckage inside white waves. She was a storm.

Elora thought she would go through the floorboards and pictured her femurs splitting as she pushed like a drill through the ground. She wanted it. She wanted the pain.

"Come on!" she shouted. Higher and harder she jumped, until her hands could smack against the ceiling, until her breath spiked her lungs and she had to quit in order to breathe. Her collection had been flung and scattered across the room. Quickly she jumped down on the floor, scooped the items into the box, slammed it shut and pushed it under the bed.

From then on, whenever the box entered her mind, she immediately shoved it out, though sometimes it wouldn't leave graciously. Sometimes it beckoned her to sit upon the bed with her knees under her chin, perched like a hawk, over her evidence. She could feel it burning under her. See? You were there. You were there, it seemed to say. There is proof that you existed in another light.

She put her hand under the bed and moved it around until she reached its cool hard surface. She pulled it out, dusted it off with toilet paper and carried it like a baby in the crook of her elbow to the door.

She stopped and looked in the mirror, with one hand she pinched her cheeks until they went pink and then pressed her fingertips into her eyes for a few moments. When she opened them she saw fuzzy black spots, she waited to regain a clear picture of herself, before she slammed the door shut.

53

The café was crowded but she needed to eat breakfast. She poked her fried egg with her fork and its sun spilt a golden puddle across her white plate. She looked out the window at the other windows, each as gray-rimmed and shadowed as tired eyes. The city pushed its steel wave against her.

A garbage truck beeped while empty bins bounced back to their places on the pavement and drivers shouted unrecognizable words. Chains scraped and clanked against the concrete. In the café, sausages and pancakes sizzled. People murmured and newspapers opened, shook, folded and tucked under arms in tan overcoats. Someone coughed a phlegmy cough then lit a cigarette. The waitress rustled as she walked, her thick knees rubbed in their pantyhose. She wiped her thumb across her blue apron, the smudge like a red cloud against a dusk sky. Water hit the burner and the coffee pot popped.

Elora held her cup with both hands and blew. Steam entered her nose. Steam reached her empty stomach before the coffees acidic swish. She leaned over and ate her egg. The morning's light was different, it was a bright washed yellow, and the sky had cleared. After so many days of hot suffocating rain it felt revolutionary. She lifted her finger and ordered toast.

Outside the sun was white and glared off the hubcaps of her car, causing her eyes to water as she fumbled for her keys. The smell of the sun warming the asphalt made her feel nauseous. She walked through the clear vapor shimmering above the parking lot towards her car carrying a polystyrene cup full of coffee and a map tucked under her arm, which she unfolded over the hood of her car. She took the address Birdie had given her out of her pocket and ran her finger up the highway parallel to the Mississippi and stopped when she reached Pine Creek, Ontario.

54.

Pine Creek, Ontario

Jacques was in his workroom when the doorbell rang. He stood up and registered the sound. A doorbell. He had forgotten he had a doorbell. He put his knife down, pulled a sheet over the figure that lay on his workbench and walked into the kitchen.

A young policeman squinted through the window. His solemn face made Jacques hesitate. He felt light-headed as if stepping off the tightrope of Before and into the free-fall of After. There was a second of midair before he reached the door; he held his breath and suspended.

"Hello, I'm looking for Jacques Beaumont?" He straightened his spine.

"I'm Jacques Beaumont."

The officer had heard he was a sculptor and a recluse. He looked at his hands. They were split along the creases, calloused and blunt like ugly sausages. Jacques lifted one up and ruffled sawdust out of his hair.

"Sorry, occupational hazard," he said. "Can I help you?"

"Mr. Beaumont, I'm John Andersen, with the Police Department," he took a badge from his breast pocket and showed it to him. "Mr. Beaumont is there anyone at home with you?"

"No, just me."

"Do you mind if I come in?"

"After you." He made a sweeping gesture with one hand and stepped aside. "I need a cup of tea, would you like one?" Jacques asked as he placed the kettle on the stove.

The kitchen walls and cupboards were painted white. The floors and countertops were wooden. A table made from an old door and two sawhorses was pushed against a bare window. The table was covered with palm-sized wooden circles stacked in rows like collapsed dominos. A book was open to a page of writing he'd never seen before.

"No thank you. I'm fine," he said.

He found that uniform pleasantries were the worst part of job. They both watched the kettle until it whistled. He wouldn't have made a cup of tea if he'd known John would decline. He couldn't stand the officer snooping over his work.

"That's Sanskrit. It's for a project I'm working on. Each word is a symbol of sorts, a meditation. I sculpt," he said taking the spoon out of his mug and placing it in the sink.

"I know," John said and Jacques arched his eyebrows in surprise. "I mean, I

197

gathered as much from all the sculptures outside."

"Ah, detective work," Jacques said.

"If only all detective work were so obvious," John laughed.

Jacques took the milk from the fridge and mixed into his tea.

"Let's talk in the living room. I don't want anything said in front of my medallions," he said and pointed to the wooden circles on the table. "Wood absorbs."

It took John a moment to realize that he was serious. He followed him through a hallway lined with overstuffed bookshelves. Jacques carried his steamy mug of tea like an extinguished candle and sat on the edge of a tan sofa, placing the mug on his knee. John sat across from him on a blue recliner. It was the only other piece of furniture in the room, no pictures, no television, no curtains, no nothing. Jacques knew what John was thinking.

"Renunciation," Jacques blew into his mug and took a drink. "So I resist distractions. Now. What have you come to tell me?"

"Right. Well," John cleared his throat and took a manila envelope out of his breast pocket. "It's difficult, but I'm here to speak to you about Nora Beaumont."

He nodded slowly. "My mother." The kestrel, he thought.

"Yes," he said allowing the word space enough to sink, then removed a few sheets of paper from the envelope.

"I understand how hard this must be Mr. Beaumont, but I do need to go over a few things with you. It says here in the file that she was suffering from dementia when she disappeared?"

"That's correct."

"And you reported her missing on April 14th 1952?"

"Yes."

"And you've had no contact with her since then?"

"No, none." He could feel his mouth line with the saliva that precedes vomit.

"Well, there's really no easy way to tell you this Mr. Beaumont but we've found her remains."

Her remains. I remain, he thought. I am all that remains of her, of a time so long ago it feels like never. He's spent years designing an alternative story for that time and now the truth, flung out before him like a writhing being, as though she were born again.

"I'm so sorry Mr. Beaumont. Here," he handed him a tissue from his pocket.

Jacques took it. "I knew she was dead. It's been years, so of course I knew it, but all the same. You have no idea." He did not sob. He caught the tears that spilled down his cheeks with the tissue.

He had carried the guilt of his relief. He wasn't proud of it, but it was true. When she finally left he had felt relieved, as though he had been wearing the wrong skin and could take it off and set it down. He thought he could come out of himself and simply walk away, but she had felt like a small animal in his hands. He never forgot. And now his mother was telling him that it was over. That he was forgiven.

"Mr. Beaumont," John's voice was a trained softness as he handed him another tissue.

"It was a freak storm."

"Mr. Beaumont, it's in the file, you don't need to explain."

"No. I do. The snow was heavy and her tracks were everywhere. Like a rabbit, you know? Zigzagged like that. She was frail by then, unreachable, one day there, the next day, gone. Just like that," he snapped his fingers. "I did what I had to do."

"Of course you did Mr. Beaumont. It would have been dangerous to go after her in those conditions. You did the right thing. You reported her absence and got on with your life."

Jacques looked at John. He knew nothing, nothing. He was a dweller of a single dimension. The type that looked at a hand and saw only a hand, not a tool that could build, that could create life, or take it away.

"Where did they find her?"

"In a ravine not far from here," John said and scratched his knee. His sympathy was waning. He coughed and his breath smelt of sweet digested coffee.

"Do you know who found her?"

"A group of hikers, geology students actually. Amazing what you can study these days. It's heavily wooded up there, as you know, anyway one slipped and fell down the ravine. He broke his leg and, incidentally, discovered your mother."

"That must have been a shock."

"Yes. I'm sure it was. Listen, Mr. Beaumont, there is something else. It was raining and Matt, the student, saw a cave along the bottom of the rock face. He dragged himself there to wait for the paramedics. That's where he found her."

As a child Jacques had named that ravine the Bandit Trap because it was hidden by snowdrifts in the winter and covered with vine in the summer. You had to fall into it to know it was there. He hadn't known about the cave. He looked out the window towards the forest. It pressed and threatened the house like a green and black glacier and he felt the split of erosion, of time. Maybe she crawled, he consoled himself, but it was a lie. In his heart he knew. He knew she'd been moved.

"It appears they were brought there by an animal and, well, I need to tell you that they've been tampered with."

"Tampered with?"

"There are, ah, quite a few post-mortem claw marks, mostly on the larger bones, made by a bear or possibly a cougar, it's hard to be absolutely certain. Mr. Beaumont, I'm so sorry, I really am. It's just dreadful after all this time. Do you have any questions?"

He thought of her piled up inside the cave like a game of pick-up sticks. He remembered her falling, how her white dressing gown had caught in the wind and for a moment she'd begun to rise, again glowing in the moonlight like a paper lantern. Her defiance included gravity. It made him breathless still.

"Can I have them? Her bones I mean, for a proper burial?"

"I'm sure that won't be a problem. Although it might take some time, you know, with the paperwork and all. I'll phone you in a week or so. Is there anything else I can do for you? Anyone I can call?"

"No. No, thank you," he said and John stood to leave. Jacques walked him to the door. A pheasant shrieked outside. The sun had dropped.

"Looks like it's going to be a nice evening," John said instead of goodbye. He wanted to leave him with something positive, poor man, out here all on his own. John was grateful he had his wife Martha at home. Life wasn't fair sometimes, he thought, but you can't help everyone. He opened the car door.

"She would hate to be boxed up," Jacques stepped out onto the porch and called after him.

"I beg your pardon?" John stood with the door open. The wind spun a pine-shaped air freshener from his rearview mirror.

"She would hate to be in some laboratory somewhere, boxed up and tagged, she'd want to be here. In this soil. Under this sky," he pointed to the clouds.

"Okay Mr. Beaumont. I understand. I'll do my best to get her home as soon as possible," he stepped into the police car. He was already thinking about what Martha might be cooking up at home.

"Thank you," Jacques said and raised one hand to say goodbye. John lifted a finger from his steering wheel.

Jacques watched the police car shrink until it was the size of a bug. Perception is everything, he thought, and walked back to his workroom and lifted the sheet from Elora.

It made sense that his mother would arrive first, he thought as he laid his hand on Elora's wooden torso.

He had found this particular log for Elora the morning after a thunderstorm. It had been a night of terrific calamity, but the morning was cool and smooth as a rock scraped clean of its moss. The morning stayed pressed against his cheeks even after he'd entered the forest. It was difficult walking, as many trees had been struck or wind torn and their limbs lay scattered everywhere. He had adapted an old sledge attached to a chest harness to help him pull out logs. The wood for his larger sculptures often arrives this way. It's hard work that he finds incredibly satisfying. He wants to build relationships that will last with his Elora's and has moved beyond frivolous, easy commitments. He hopes he has given her a sustenance that's meaningful.

Anyone who has spent time with trees knows that each one has a different personality, so when he's searching for a piece to sculpt, he's also searching for a tree that can cope with change. Some simply can't, some roots are too deep and want to die and feed the soil to which they were born. He respects that. He leaves them for the beetles and searches for the logs that secretly wish they were birds.

She was in a clearing, lightning-struck and still smoldering on the ground like a fallen warrior. He touched her and sensed her bravery, her flight and her bird dreams. She sighed when he sawed off her damage, she fell asleep as if to convalesce, and he saw the woman within, her face creased inside the bark like a face pressed against glass. At once, he recognized it as Elora and although he has been carving her for two years now, he had never seen the face that she'd resuscitated. It meant that she was close, and although it was what he wanted, the idea of her arrival left him unable to move, unable to speak. He just stood there and let the past land on him, all at once, a flock of birds and it was deafening.

*

He was a sculptor that removed. That's what he did. He cut, he shaved and sanded away all that was unnecessary (however luscious, however fleshy) from his object until it had the required space to open. Like years that eat away at a memory, like ants that eat a fruit, entirely, until they reach the stone, the truth, the seed. Each sculpture was a seed and with this one he'll plant Elora. Again.

*

He gives new life to the fallen, an artistic decomposing because wood was always changing, always moving and, for years, remained alive. He liked the fact that it was only the solidity, not his marks, that could remain permanent. It filled him with a strange hope. Nobody wants the full truth, like a pause, it weighs too much.

He caught them at their heaviest. It was a service really, a bit like a chaperone or a bellhop. If you broke art, if you broke death down, it was ordinary. He painted X while eating toast. X died after making a bank deposit. The ordinary facts were the most haunting. One reason for this was because they hid the creator, the exterminator, the devil in the details. The other reason was because they brought the unimaginable close enough to recognize.

Always in the wood he recognized the tree, the thing it had been, which was already a measure of perfection that he didn't dare to compete with, like life and its perfect design, his art was the other side to the story, the other face. There is never only one. The idea of one perception is impossible, so each tree was also designed for the body that he gave it, a secret longing perhaps, an underbelly, the thought churning inside it as changing as erosion.

It is a type of love in the way that it cannot be sequestered. It belongs to him, is vital to him and this idea pleases him as he imagines a companion might. He has many things in common with his father. The main thing being that they both shared a need to physically hold their feelings through a created object. Jacques detached to visualize, then recreated, the parts of himself that he needed to understand. He was a tactile man. He needed to hold his emotions, cut, mold, chisel and rearrange them so that he could control them. Sometimes he imagined that he sculpted himself out of form and into nothing, a zip of light that simply burned to black. The thought was both sustaining and horrible.

55

Elora followed the Mississippi north along a stretch of highway. She opened the windows and concaved her brain. Her photographs hung from her mind like a row of drying hides, rawhide, she thought as the wind slapped against them as a thumb across cards. Few things allow the mind to detour like driving. She likes to sit in the middle of windows, likes to speed to the end of the city and will the countryside to move. It makes her feel linear when she is otherwise not. Sometimes you need to move towards the bull's-eye, she thought. He won't recognize her like this. He won't recognize her with influence.

*

The sunlight snapped off behind the door and her hotel room immediately became a cave, dark, damp, orange and brown. So much for cheap and cheerful. A musty womb, she thought and stroked her stomach. Her body seemed alien, as though it were making decisions without her.

The heating was on and the air stung her eyes, so she flicked the heater off and tried to open the window, but found it was nailed shut. She opened the front door and switched on the bathroom fan, it clicked like a card in a bicycle wheel, which made the room seem nervous. She peeled the bedspread from the bed, threw it in the corner, and then sat down inside a swarm of dust motes floating in a stream of sun like gnats.

The fan kept clicking. She took off her shoe, threw it at the fan and to her surprise the clicking stopped. Her car's engine was cooling, more clicking. It was parked right outside the door. There were bugs splattered on the grill and behind that a pink neon vacancy sign flashed against a cloudless blue sky. Everywhere glared. A fly buzzed through the door and, gratefully, back out again. She needed a moment to relax, so straightened her back and sat motionless.

Then caught and slowed her breathing until it moved in a continuous circle. Take in. Give out. A chill ran down her neck and softened her shoulders. She felt the hot air encase her and a breeze touch her sweaty face like a fingertip. She gently stopped her mind and brought it back to sensation, the feeling of her sweat, the movement of her breath, the sound of birds, passing cars, electricity, footsteps and someone unlocking the next door.

She opened the curtains and turned on the air conditioning. She smelled her armpit. She needed a shower.

The bathroom light sputtered to a dull hum and made her face look yellow, prickled even, her cheeks like a plucked chicken's breast. When she moved to the city she had her hair cut short. She ran her fingers through her hair and it felt like stroking a tabby cat. She turned on the shower and while she waited for the water to warm, she looked in the mirror and touched her face as if actualizing herself as real, pulling and pushing, with her fingers she broke her face into shapes.

Nose: as slender as a finger with a bottom heavy triangle. Cheeks: two sharp half cylinders. Eyes: two white rings, two gray rings and two black circles. Lips: slanted line, inverted triangle, slanted line, crescent. Forehead: three permanent creases between her eyes. Chin: dented vertical oval. To see a face is to feel it. True faces are felt, she thought, otherwise they're lies. The mirror began to steam, inside the shower, she dissolved.

Elora stepped from the shower and smoothed her hair with her hands as she entered the bedroom. The cool air hits her damp body. She got into bed and hid under the covers. The eroticism of wet skin on the bed sheet strangely aroused her as she lay there straining her ears to hear the soothing growl of semi-trucks tunneling their steel frames down the highway of an isolated night.

It sounded like what she wanted, sounded like freedom, a way to break free, new words to use, not these words. These words hung on the walls of her mind, black letters on white canvases, parts in a jar, preserving her, illustrating her. She was a collection of erratic meanings. She tried to piece them together, to fill in the holes. She tries to remember Jacques's face by painting it in her mind: oval with cheekbones jutted as sticks, a deep dimple in his chin, broad nose, but when she stands back to view him, it is herself she sees on the canvas and a single black word: loneliness. Loneliness. Broad as the break of day, any day. All her days were the same, shoulder touching shoulder until they stopped, until they burned, like paper dolls, ablaze.

*

That night she dreamed a highway lay across her body. It began on her forehead, spread over her nose, lips and chin, and then ran across her chest and stomach. At her throat and her pelvis it branched into two and stretched down her arms and legs. In her dream she kept driving and driving along herself. Above her, bulbous cartoon clouds sped across a blue sky, a cartoon sun and moon exchanged in seconds, and day quickened to night and back again. Time rushed outside her window and she was alone in her car whizzing down the empty highway with grass-bending force. A steel finger parting hair.

56.

The birds were singing when she woke. She got up and put on her jeans, white button down shirt and stood in front of the window. She stretched her arms towards the warm sun like a plant and the sun streamed into her as if her body were a shot-up target the light shone through. She was hungry. She went to the bathroom and brushed her teeth, grabbed her hotel key, slipped on her loafers and left.

The hotel was attached to a small café and Elora quickly slid into a high-backed pleather booth by the window and spread the map out on the table. It was flabbergasting how close Jacques had been. Two days drive away. She could easily reach his house by this evening, but had decided to back track to Callisto and photograph Arlo. There was spilled salt on the table and she threw a few grains over her shoulder.

"Superstitious, huh?" said the waitress arriving with a cloth to wipe the table.

"It's an old habit," said Elora. She noticed the waitress's name was Sandy; she was probably in her forties.

"That's better. Can I get you a drink?"

"Coffee and water please."

"Are you ready to order food too?"

"I think I'll just have a slice of coconut cream pie."

"Sure thing; be right back."

Across the road was a fenced field like any other. Cattle stared at her while they slowly chewed, their jaws constantly grinding, turning. She had missed the infinite expanses of land and sky. The unevenness of the pulled apart clouds as if the sky were denim too long in the sun and bleached along its creases.

The sky in Chicago was always spiked with metal's posture, building, bridge, crane, all screaming a separation from the natural world. She knew the buildings to climb that offered the most uninterrupted views, like steel and glass pedestals of restoration. Lake Michigan had offered an indifferent respite, but it was tidal and crashed, whereas the Mississippi rolled. She had always been a sky and river person.

She had died alongside the Mississippi. The thought of Arlo and her old life no longer asphyxiated her. The woman who had sung beside the river and even the thought of Jacques, had begun to recede into the obscure briars of her memory.

She had also been reborn alongside the Mississippi. For better or for worse, Jacques had wanted her to live, so here she was, inside this strange, hollowed body for which she documented emotion.

Photographing Arlo would chronicle justice.

57

When she reached the turning for Callisto, she drove off the main highway and down the back roads towards the side entrance to her Father's old land. She drove until she saw an iron gate at the top of a grassy hill. She parked the car alongside the road and began to climb, swatting mayflies from her face. Crossing the field and following the track would take her to the other side of the river, where there were trees, rocky outcrops and coves full of fish. During this time of year, she would certainly find Arlo. Photographing him on the Mississippi seemed appropriate, plus he was trapped on the boat and wouldn't be able to reach or hurt her.

The abandoned house was long gone but the rhubarb was growing wild as anything. Elora sat on a stagecoach stump at the top of the hill. It was another five minute walk to the river and she could see it snaking through the trees. It must have been a beautiful spot to settle.

Beside the house was a little cemetery surrounded by a rusted gate and fence. Cemeteries like this could be found up and down the wagon trail. Elora knew to look for the telltale iron gate poking through a grove of scrappy pines planted to keep the soil from eroding. Not many were this lucky of course, most had only wooden crosses or just stones to mark their passing. Elora pictured the wind whipping off the layers of soil covering their frail bones like sheets, lost in the wind they disintegrated, funneled and swirled like insects in a current, then vanished. Time is lost in places like this; time means nothing.

She thought of her old life and herself as a child.

In her childhood bedroom there had been a single window. On stormy nights the wind softly rattled the oval mirror above her wooden dresser. Apart from her bed she had no other furniture, just a denim rag rug and a gold hook on the back of her door. Every other inch of space was covered with magpie objects, feathers, sticks, acorns, rocks, egg shells, a piece of foil she'd found on the grass like a fallen star. Objects man had named inanimate, bones. But it's not true, for if she stared hard enough, mindfully enough, the inanimate became animate. Became a song. The rock grew a face and the chipped bone, a new skin. She digested their curves and they charted one another, became maps of the same landscape, kin. In black marker she wrote her favorite words on the walls. Then she sang them alive.

Now she could do the opposite.

She remembered the day her Father returned home from hospital. The doctors had told him his cancer was irreparable. The afternoon light had already begun to muddy the stark yellow of morning. She watched the air thicken, watched the shadows lengthen in silence. Silence was everywhere and it filled her. Her eyes shifted through its coating like two stealth swimmers parting water, she pored over things: a white door handle, a glass vase on the dresser holding pheasant feathers, a watermark in the ceilings right corner that looked like a starfish or a smudged handprint. Outside a gust of wind shook the dust from the leaves thin backs. A branch scraped the window. The knowledge that life was impermanent filled her mind like lungs inhaling air. He died within a year.

In Chicago, she sat at the window and watched the city hit against the night like a shine across black leather. She'd stare and listen to sounds trickle through a darkness haloed by streetlights, damp headlights and a few other yellowed windows. Pure black existed only in patches, in parks, down alleyways and corners, black crevices where sound and light slowed and labored as if rolling through tar, a cough, a pair of lit eyes, cold cardboard. Elsewhere light burned through black, fusing and reinventing black as watered-down amethyst, dark gold and army green bruises. Sometimes she'd light a candle just to see her shadow pulse. To remind her of her power. Sometimes the wind blew her shadow, banging like a dark hand against the wall and she'd stare at things until she no longer reacted to them. All night stripping objects of their names.

In the city she spent summer afternoons in the park under a particular tree; she'd sit watching its pale green leaves oxidize to gray. She always left at dusk, so never saw the leaves turn black with night, but pictured them often just before sleep, saw their yellow light draining to uncover an opaque figure, like a sunlit puddle evaporating to divulge its solid mud bottom. The person she had become.

It was time to say goodbye to her old self now.

She followed the track to the trees, sat on the riverbank and waited for Arlo's boat to appear. The reeds harped inside the mud and swallows dipped and caught early evening bugs. Across the water, the skeletal remains of Jacques burnt-out house settled into the landscape like a rotting corpse. In the distance, Birdie's house and the grave of her and Jacque's dead child, Lorelei. She took a photo of the grave. A shot from a distance was best, and then Elora closed her eyes and reveled in the synchronization of knowing that she was putting events to rest.

Before long, Arlo's boat retched through the air. Geese flapped up in warning. She stood to face him. The engine oil was pungent as he motored into view. Look at me, she beckoned him, and he did. When he saw her standing there, like a ghost, he cut the engine and lunged forward, but the boat nearly capsized and forced him to steady himself. She smiled, waved and brought the camera up to her eye.

She took photo after photo, capturing him inside the negative. He shook his head to remove her image. There was nothing he could do to hurt her now. He looked as silly as a toad. It was stupid how simple it was. Stupid. To make it ceremonious would add a gravitas he didn't deserve. Within minutes, the current floated him downstream and out of view. She put the camera down and walked back to the car. The sunset now was thick and red as flayed muscles through the trunks of trees. This is the first life she has truly owned.

58.

Back in the hotel, she stood in the bath, the water was so hot that she had to enter inch by inch, her ears were the last to submerge. The water cupped her face like two steaming hands. She could hear her body digesting, gurgling, she heard what her blood heard. She heard what her child had heard. Few noises are as indiscriminately human.

She thought of the city and how dawn played it like a beautiful tragedy. She remembers moving through it. She would leave her apartment like entering an empty theater, the play over, the forgotten applause still cracking its speechless noise in the air. She could hear the slightest shift, her eyes drew long gazes, her breath lengthened. The first thing she always noticed was the waste, so much waste. Garbage bins spilled over like leaky bouquets: uneaten food, piled, picked through and rat nibbled. The homeless with red cauliflower noses, thick blue ankles, some with clothes stuffed with bags to soften the night's blows, like forgotten ragged teddy bears, or others like stick insects with skeletal feet inside large shoes, wrapped in dirty blankets and dogs – she could feel them awake, waiting, needing.

And then, a reminder of love.

Some mornings she would walk to the park and sit on the same bench with coffee in hand, watching ordinary humans rush to work. One morning a couple appeared around the corner, laughing. They kissed in front of the duck pond before heading in different directions. It was a deep kiss, it was not a kiss that was meant to shock, it was natural and true, when all around them everybody pushed and frowned.

She knew it was voyeuristic and odd to watch, but she found it so promising how they dissolved the anonymity of the city like salt on a slug. To witness their open intimacy felt encouraging and soon she began to notice the things that made them uniquely beautiful, like how his tie was tied too short or how her shoe scuffed, her nose was flat, his ears were big. That's how love was meant to be. She had never loved in the open. Until now, her heart had lived in secrecy. Photography allowed her to expose herself.

What is beautiful, what is human, is unpolished and visible.

It was not a new idea, but as it entered Elora, it felt fresh, even comforting. She understood that there were only a handful of truly meaningful ideas, but what she found miraculous was our ability to continually feel them anew.

Jacques had wanted an entirely numinous life. But that was just nostalgia for a time lived or unlived, for he never understood that what lasts as beauty is incredibly normal. Falling down, scraping your face, being late for work, cooking, screwing, crapping, eating. Normal humans are traitors, dreamers, wasters. They envy, scheme, long, forgive. He only wanted what shimmered, but there must be a balance, otherwise the shimmer is too bright or the mundane too burdensome.

Could they share a life with their respective abilities or were they destined to live alone?

Could she forgive him for how he had created her?

She pulled the plug out with her toe and lay still while the water drained. By the time she reached for her towel, the skin on her stomach was cold and dry. She dried her hair and crawled into bed, like any normal person she thought, in the unreal world and dreamed.

*

A dream of a frail girl with hair chopped and uneven as a head of lettuce. She stood on a flat rock in the middle of a pond. Dragonflies with slick aquamarine backs slide through the air around her in giant, then small, then giant circles. They flicked their prehistoric bodies towards the sun with blue phosphorus and brilliant flashes, then withdrew, became invisible but for steady hums in the air.

The girl was naked. In each hand she held a bucket, her pale muscles strained, her skin was crimson from the sun. Elora called out to her. Take this shirt, she said, take this blanket. Then the strangest thing happened, the girl began to yodel, high and loud and echoing. Elora could see the sounds, the music notes as they left her mouth, swirling cartoon notes, red and rising, they pierced and bent the bones in Elora's ears. She screamed for her to stop, but the girl sang louder and louder until her voice cracked. The bones in Elora's ears snapped and a warm liquid slid down her neck.

Her skin began to deepen with color, the sun was relentless with its glare, the sun stared at them, beat them, when suddenly the girl let out one string of laughter and then burst into flames. Elora screamed for her to jump. Jump in the water! Jump in the water! She begged her to jump into the water. She did not, so Elora started swimming towards her but she couldn't swim hard enough, fast enough. The flames crackling, cracking, were taking her. Elora could no longer see her face, could no longer see the contours of her body, it was melting, her body was melting off her and Elora was afraid to look, but kept swimming, kept swimming, kept trying to swim.

Then the fire abruptly ended. She was gone. She had vanished. Small bits of ash fell gracefully from the sky and landed on the rock. It was silent enough to hear the trees stop and stir and stop again and the water rippled with the wind. Like a circle growing larger and larger a wave gained force and threw itself over the rock cleaning it of her ashes. The buckets the girl had held floated to a marshy cove, branch covered and cool with moss. Elora looked and saw hundreds and hundreds of white buckets stacked upon one another, resting, with wet frogs jumping in and out of their white round mouths. She did not belong here. A silent terror surged though her. The world was terribly quiet, but for the sudden splash of frog and the hit of each wave. Spatter spray spatter spray. There were no birds.

She did not belong here.

The mere shape of her body was loud, the pale color of her skin was intrusive. She climbed up on the rock and noticed her clothes were missing, noticed that she was holding two buckets, unable to move and petrified of speaking, of making a sound, of burning, she looked inside the buckets and was blinded by the white flames they contained.

She opened her eyes and sat up in bed. On the walls, the hotel paintings hung, lonely as dark ships. The headlights of passing cars lapped against each canvas. The bed was a soft white island that she sunk back into; it was only a dream, a dream.

Everything has changed and nothing at all.

She had just begun living on the outside, but the altering, the real work of turning the heart around, had occurred months ago, years, had begun a thousand years ago, perhaps had not stopped its churning, its blending of lost and gained. The truth had been spoken and a grip released. Suddenly she had found herself a loose balloon in the wind. She could see her red self floating. She knew she could end up anywhere, this was the danger; the danger was the ecstasy.

59.

She stops the car in Lake Itasca, sixty miles outside of Pine Creek. The road is empty all the way to the mountains. Lake Itasca is the headwater of the Mississippi. She leaves the car and walks to the edge of the glacial lake where the river begins. Thick pines along the sides and boulders rolling all the way to the shoreline. She sits on a large rock and dangles her feet inside the cold water. The clouds are mirrored across the waters surface. She holds the cigar box in her lap, removes a silver locket from its contents, and fastens it around her neck. It had belonged to her mother.

She wished for a child to inherit it.

Everything else inside the box belongs to another woman. She folded her map to fit, placed it inside with a few heavy rocks and shut the lid. To keep yourself open is on some level to submerge to a close, like coral closes inside of water, and is most beautiful when left undisturbed. Life, love are disturbing, inspirational, yes, but disturbing all the same. Maybe he had never loved her enough to be interrupted. Maybe he only wanted to interrupt. Well, she was the result of his interruption.

The moon was a small C in the sky. The air off the water smelt like cool wet leaves. The mountains perched in the far-off distance like hawks.

She removed a piece of rope from her pocket and tied the rope tightly around the box so that it looked like a present. A present for the river. Then, she pitched the box into the air as hard as she could, it flew for a second before cutting straight through the water, and it barely made a ripple. In her mind she watched it sink quickly to the bottom and lodge firmly in the brown mud, and once the cloud of mud and a few scared fish cleared away the box looked as if it has always been there.

That is what her body would have done before the gas of her decay rose her to the surface. That woman needs to stay here now, she tells herself, here below the mouth of the river is where she belongs.

Above it the river moved on and on and she sat there for a long time breaking back to nothing.

She thought back to that night. She would have died alongside the river. She did die alongside the river, but then she rose from it again. The first step, he had orchestrated, but every other step had been of her making.

Her thoughts scattered like gulls. Her seagulls, the birds he had heard. She let them. She let them go and watched as they disappeared. She could feel, inside of herself, a silence pulling down like a root, a quiet knowing. Sometimes a need will go on so long that it becomes a grind that must turn itself out of you like a screw, like this, twisting through tailbone and out the balls of her feet. The resulting pattern is a coiled cavern where a new trust, like a cool stream begins to lick the splintered edges smooth. She let herself feel it and closed her eyes, and breathed into herself.

*

It was nearly dawn, but still dark when she left. The river was a metal gray, the sky was cold and hazy. She noticed a round rock similar in shape and size to a geode and when she looked closer she saw that there were many, clustered like black mushrooms, wet and musty. They seemed real. She watched them as they slowly begin to pinken into a patch of bald heads under the light of the suns golden eyelid as it opened up the distance with its red lashes.

She chose the rock closest to her and carried it back to her car and placed it on the passenger seat. She had the strange sense that it was living. She had felt this way about eggs before, as if they were asking to hatch. She knew a person that could help her crack it. When this was over, she will contact Birdie and thank her.

She started her car and drove away. It was the only car on the road. The lights on her speedometer faded as the sun came up. We are the chances we take, she said, and it felt like a mantra. The window down; the hair on her arms standing up. She could feel her chest leap; she leapt. She felt.

She drove slowly down Jacques's lane so as not to wake him. She parked, picked up the wooden sculpture of Callisto, closed the car door very carefully and walked towards the porch.

Elora didn't rush, instead she concentrated on placing each heel precisely in front of the opposite toe, linking her footprints to trail a chain behind her. The house was quiet, and she knew when she reached it everything would change for this is what happens when pieces slide into place; they plow and unearth a rough terrain.

The garden was full of sculptures, she entered the fold, walked in and out and around their bodies. They were magnificent. Each of them had a feature that moved in the wind, arms that swung or rope hair, their eyes were painted stones. They were without grime and spotless. Most of them looked similar to her. It was like walking through her montage.

She stood in the middle of the women and watched the sun come up from behind the house to warm the sky, watched clouds roll behind the trees, break into kaleidoscopes and emerge whole again. The leaves had begun to turn colors, like orange ink spilling across the green, like leaky red veins through the pine's thick bodies. She would have liked to watch the color spread, deciding she wanted nothing more than to see a cycle complete itself.

It's amazing how one circumstance, one hour, can reconstruct a lifetime, and while the moment is performing, we sit on the cusp of our own definition, isolated by magnitude and inert in time.

It was bath day. He walked down the steps with soapy water and linseed oil. One of his statues caught his eye and started walking slowly towards him. Elora. He stepped down from the porch. He was wearing an oilcloth apron and had long yellow gloves on. He dropped the bucket and the water ran down the steps. He didn't care or notice.

He whispered her name.

60.

She walked closer to him. Her flowered dress in the breeze, her laced up boots on the grass, she coughed, she was real, his head began to spin, he leaned against the banister and she reached out her hand, as though to catch him. He dropped to the ground. She knelt beside him.

There seemed nothing and everything to say, as if one word, one single word, would act like a crack in the levee and they would drown. The soapy water soaked into the soil. He began popping the bubbles, he touched her forehead with a wet finger to make sure she didn't disappear.

"You're alive," he said. "I can't believe you're here."

"I am," she said and stood. "And you, too, are alive. I've brought you something," she handed him the carving of Callisto. He took it and stared at her.

He brought it to his nose and smelled it. "Callisto?" His face was shocked. "Where did you get this?"

"On the kitchen table, where you left it," she said.

"Where I left it?"

"Yes. It was there the morning after you died, or left, or whatever the hell you did. After you changed me."

"I didn't die. And I didn't change you, I resurrected you, I saved you," he said.

"I see that," she interrupted.

"And I didn't leave this. It isn't mine," he said searching the grain of the bear.

"What? Whose was it then?"

He began to pry off the head.

"Stop it! You'll break it," she said as the bear head popped off in his hand. Inside its torso was a small folded piece of paper. A white mushroom inside the knot of a tree. A white moth under a log.

"It's my father's," he said unfolding the note. "It has to be; he left it for me," he trembled as he lowered onto the wet soil and read the poem.

Down the Mountainside
For you,
I tie a limb
in a bow
around a heavy rock, that knotted,
that tight

ball of string,
for you, son,
I'll let myself
go.
"Tell me what happened after I left," he said.

*

The stories they exchanged were not so different from the ones they'd made up inside themselves. Their child, his father, victims of place and time. When people share a death they often share a rebirth. He took her to the sculpture of his mother.

"I knew she was returning and she did. I have the power of resurrection," he waved a hand towards his garden of goddesses. "You came back to me."

"I came here to see if you were alive and to tell you that I, too, create things. Photographs," she said.

"Photographs? You're a photographer?" He looked at her and down at the sculpture of Callisto.

"Yes."

"Of course," he smiled. "Of course. Show me."

61.

He helped her bring them in from the car and hung them on the walls of his living room. He took some other photographs from the closet, pictures of bears, himself as a child, the mountains and his mother. He hung them beside hers. He circled around her photos, asking what each symbol meant. She found herself describing a person she admired, however despicable, and this surprised her.

"They are magnificent," he said.

"They are just true," she said.

"No. Not just. More than that. They hide the truth by revealing it. It's what I do. It's what my father did," he stood in silence for a while. "I can't believe he actually came for me. All this time I thought his body was on the mountain. I've even thought I've felt him as I harvest the wood. I assumed he had finally met his bear, and so, I didn't try to resurrect him," his eyes brimmed with tears.

"There is no way you could have known. His spirit was free because you didn't resurrect him. And you probably have felt him in the woods, because his spirit went where it wanted to be," she put her hand on his shoulder.

"And you," he looked up at her. "Are you where you want to be?"

"When I was alive, I wanted to sing and be near you, so in that way, yes, I suppose, but I don't know now. I'm not the same person. It's hard to know what you want when you have to learn how to feel. I'm still adjusting."

"I wish I could say I was sorry, but I'm not. You are standing here in front of me, without fear or secrecy, you can become whomever you want and Arlo will never hurt you again," he went to hug her, but she pulled away.

"Do you really think it was your father that Arlo murdered?" She avoided his touch.

"It has to be. Somehow Arlo killed my father instead of me and I wasn't there," he looked out the window towards his father's work shed.   He would carve his father as a bear. Rage and its slow eternal burn, charred his inside, he would finish his father's sculpture.

"If you would have been there, then we both would be dead, and anyway, you can't be sure that Arlo killed him."

"I can and I am. He carved animals for me when he went away on expedition. I left him the encyclopedia as a clue and he left me Callisto. The bear's name is Callisto. That's why I moved there in the first place. He figured it out and he came for me. You saw the photo's of my father, we looked very similar."

"What will you do?"

"I'll let fate decide."

"What does that mean?"

"It means that I know where there are some eyes in the forest that can help us."

"What kind of fairytale bullshit is that?"

"It's not bullshit, it's a plant. Actaea pachypoda. Also known as 'Doll's Eye'," he said, rose from the chair and pulled the encyclopedia off the shelf, opened it to the correct page and handed her the book. The picture was of a stalk with long bristles and white berries with black pupils stuck onto their thin red stems. They were extraordinary and looked just like eyes.

"I've never seen anything like this before," she said.

"I can take you to them."

"With the right light, I could make it look like an eyeball stuck on red needle. I know that sounds a bit macabre, but in the right context, it would look astonishing."

"In the right context, I can see it."

"I could do a collage. You know, many eyes exposed to different lights, then reattached to the same stalk. Maybe I could even paint a few," she said.

"I would even make you a wooden one. You could place it alongside a real eye. Arlo's," he said.

"What?"

"I mean the eye could be Arlo's," he looked straight at her. Outside fireflies dipped in and out of his sculptures. Elora was silent.

"It could be the one that holds the mystery," he said.

"The mystery?"

"Every work of art holds the mystery of its creation close to the surface, but untraceable."

"What are you suggesting?"

"Five little eyes in a bitter wine will stop a heart that deserves stopping," he said and took a drink. "Think of the image Elora. Think of giving birth to that. You're an artist now. We both are and this man deserves to die for what he's taken from us."

She understood exactly what he meant. Understood it completely.

They stared at one other and inside the slant of windowed sun between them, grew the image of a body, as if their veins were crocheting together and creating an entirely new person.

She felt something drop inside her, cold as a seed and black as a note of music.

"There is no need for that," she said and took her camera from her bag. "I have a photo of Arlo in here. I have the ability to end him. That's what you gave me. That was my rebirthing. You resurrect. I take away. All I need is a darkroom."

When she spoke, the pieces of their future slotted into place like loose blocks of ice will freeze into a single sheet of glacier. The frost behind his eyes began again, only this time it was shared warmth. She could understand him now. They could unite. He put his hand over hers. As true partners.

"You have no idea what this means," he said and stopped. How could he finish this sentence?

"I'm still learning to feel," she said. "I don't know if I can."

When she imagined her own eyes, they were barren like soil where life had been uprooted. Holes.

"I will help you. Trust me, this is how we were meant to be," he said. "I love you. I want to learn how to love you more."

She thought about his love and it's potential hope inside her own disturbed earth. Maybe. Maybe he could fill her.

"We'll see," she removed her lens cap. "Stay like that. Don't move," she said as she placed her camera against her eye and shot his photograph.

Epilogue

Arlo sat bolt upright in bed, gasping for breath and panting in the pre-bird morning with a feeling of panic he could not explain. I'm going to die, he thought, end. There had been no nightmare, no pain, just the sense of his world being gathered up and yanked away from him as though his surroundings had been painted on cloth. For a moment he felt the fragile ripping of premonition and stared past the window frame at a windbreak of leafless trees, black branches stitched across a gray dawn. He thought of her eyebrows against her bloated forehead and shuddered.

He swore he'd seen her the other day. Like a damn ghost, he saw her near his fishing cove, but when he turned the boat around, she had gone. Vanished. He should cut back on his drinking.

Arlo was not a good man, not even a decent one, and had learned to shake off any earthly forewarnings that might force him to consider his own karmic comeuppance. There were things he was willing to contemplate and things he wasn't willing to contemplate. It was as simple as that. The past was in the past and when it showed signs of rearing its ugly head, he focused his mind on the thing he loved best, fishing.

It was early autumn and the fish would still be biting. His heart slowed as he imagined catfish waiting on the river's bottom like quiet whiskered stones. Stones that were muddied straight through to the point of putrefaction and if he had a soul, then surely, it resembled this.

There she was again.

Her white arm reaching up for him and the river, full of hooks and snags, tumbling around it like a mysterious dream. Her fingers unkempt with seaweed, her mouth opened and out floated two huge water lilies, as pink as lungs, bobbing up and down the current. Elora. He hadn't thought about her for months, and now, all of the sudden, she was everywhere.

At first, he couldn't even look at the river without imagining some part of her body resurfacing and he felt the panic of then, the anger. Why was she back now? He punched down his thoughts with action, pulled on yesterday's clothes, had a piss and went into the kitchen to pour himself a scotch. These things take more time than we realize, he thought, filled his flask and grabbed his fishing rod.

His boots broke across shards of frosty grass and his breath clouded the air. It seemed as though he were the only thing awake until his boat motor started like some faithful animal. He moved quickly across ripples.

The river's wind was a good smack across the face and cleared his mind. He took a deep breath and welcomed the return of his old self just before he was pushed into the water.

It was shocking and cold. The boat was empty and sped off without him. He tried to swim, but his body was completely frozen and inert. He could only move his eyelids and his mouth. He shouted for help and floated on his back. The current was as tangled as Elora's hair and it carried him like a log downstream. Stars raced above him, fading ornaments against the metal sky and an arrow of geese. Lines of trees shadowed the bank like a watching crowd.

He felt himself pulled under and when he screamed the water swelled into him like the sucking in of bellows. It felt purposeful as though the water were enjoying it, as though it were alive.

Lightning Source UK Ltd.
Milton Keynes UK
UKOW04f1803260917
309924UK00001B/3/P

9 780995 684379